The Last Chance Ladies' Book Club

THE LAST CHANCE LADIES' BOOK CLUB

MARLIS WESSELER

Signature
EDITIONS

Cover design by Doowah Design.
Photo of Marlis Wesseler by Don Hall.

Acknowledgements
I'd like to thank Sandra Birdsell, Connie Gault, Joan Givner, and Dianne Warren for their critical advice; the Saskatchewan Arts Board for a grant supporting this project; and my husband Lutz Wesseler for his support of all my projects in all kinds of ways.

This book was printed on Ancient Forest Friendly paper.
Printed and bound in Canada by Hignell Book Printing Inc.

We acknowledge the support of the Canada Council for the Arts and the Manitoba Arts Council for our publishing program.

Library and Archives Canada Cataloguing in Publication

Wesseler, Marlis, 1952-, author
        The Last Chance Ladies' Book Club / Marlis Wesseler.

Issued in print and electronic formats.
ISBN 978-1-77324-018-3 (softcover).
--ISBN 978-1-77324-019-0 (EPUB)

        I. Title.

PS8595 E63 L37 2017   C813'.54   C2017-904692-6
                                                C2017-904693-4

Signature Editions
P.O. Box 206, RPO Corydon, Winnipeg, Manitoba, R3M 3S7
www.signature-editions.com

to the memory of
Clara Nordin

It was a hot Sunday toward the beginning of July when Donald Eston arrived at Pleasant Manor. Eleanor happened to be right there with Fern, ready to take a walk around the block, when a station wagon pulled up at the front entrance. An elderly man sat inside, hunched like a question mark, waiting for the middle-aged driver to help him out of the vehicle.

Eleanor could see Mrs. Brown, the manager, watching from the foyer, wearing a bright turquoise pantsuit that day. As the newcomer emerged to stand hesitantly beside the car, the giant glass doors whined open and she strode over to him. Her determined heartiness always reminded Eleanor of Patsy Cline, although for all she knew Mrs. B. couldn't carry a tune. Her first name was Angela, but no one ever thought to call her that. "Hello, Mr. Eston," she called, as if he were some distance away. "Welcome to Pleasant Manor!" She shook his hand.

Hearing his name, Eleanor tried to stare only at the sidewalk as she and Fern made their way past him. They walked until they were a fair distance down the path, then both stopped at the same time and turned to look back. They must not make themselves noticeable, Eleanor thought. She couldn't let herself gape at this man, tried to keep her gaze above him, as if she were intent on watching the shades on the second floor. She gripped Fern's arm.

"So it was his furniture they were moving into Al Swenson's place the other day." Fern sounded calmer than she looked. Al Swenson had been her next-door neighbour, his death only two weeks ago. Eleanor could feel Fern's tremor become worse, moving from one to about five on her personal Richter scale. She noticed Mrs. Brown give them a concerned glance, and for an awful moment thought she was going to call them back, to introduce them to him. But she waved, friendly and dismissive, and continued to lead the man and his driver toward the building.

Eleanor leaned heavily on her cane. The ground had become unstable and for a second, she was afraid her bad knee would buckle. Even as she concentrated on remaining upright, she couldn't take her eyes off the man's back as he made his way to the entrance. He walked hunched over, but as he approached the doors was able to straighten right up, as if to give himself encouragement, and read the inscription carved into the stone archway. Eleanor had passed it so often she'd forgotten it was there: "Sisters of Our Lady of Perpetual Help, 1905." A copper plate under that said "Pleasant Manor, 1985."

The younger man returned to the car, which Eleanor knew was a Saturn because it was like the one her son Dennis owned for highway driving. Could this be Eston's son? Heavyset, he was at least a head taller than his skinny father — a block off the old chip, Orest would have said. He gave her and Fern a curious glance, and Eleanor looked down at the petunias flourishing along the path. She flicked at a dandelion with her cane, pretending to point out the weed to Fern.

Saturn. Who'd done that painting of Saturn eating his children? El Greco? Goya. Orest had once bought her a set of Great Art books, which she'd given to Dennis when she moved to Pleasant Manor. But she could remember every detail of the expression on Saturn's face, his plate-sized eyes wild with grief, cosmic nausea and gut-wrenching horror, far more worthy of being labelled human than the monster who was now entering the building.

"We should try to look normal," Fern said, moving toward the street.

"Yes. We might as well take our walk," Eleanor said. The ground was still slightly precarious, but she forced herself to move on. "We don't want anyone to see us looking as if we'd run into a ghost."

They crossed the gravel street into a green and blooming neighbourhood of pastel bungalows. Abundant rain in June had produced peonies hanging gloriously pink and ragged, some so heavy they touched the earth. Periwinkle covered excess ground, perfect lines of vegetables thrived in backyard gardens, lawns were a lush, smooth emerald. "Well, the worst has happened," Eleanor said. "He's here." A veneer of calm was taking over, covering her sense of dread, but her knee began to ache.

"Are you all right?" Fern asked, nervously touching her hair, which was tied back today in a skimpy white knot. The sleeve of her sweatshirt, Eleanor noticed in spite of her state of mind, was frayed.

"Oh, I'm fine, I just need to slow down a bit." Invisible webs brushed her face as they navigated a sidewalk lined with elm trees. Fern was so much taller that Eleanor's hand was falling asleep clutching her arm. She let go and they walked without saying anything until they were back at the Manor. "We have to tell Olivia and Thelma," Eleanor said.

They sat down to rest on a bench outside the main building for a few minutes before dinner. Although Eleanor generally cooked for herself, on weekends she and Fern met their friends Olivia and Thelma for the big Sunday meal in the dining hall.

From the bench, she had a view of several of the fourplex bungalows that radiated away from the Manor in rows like spokes from a hub. Each tiny front-garden plot was blooming with pansies, busy Lizzies, peonies, lilies, daisies, roses. A couple of the plots needed weeding. Not wanting to focus, she encouraged her thoughts to float aimlessly toward flowers and weeds.

The Saturn was parked at Al Swenson's place now, the driver lifting luggage and boxes from the back. Eston would be Fern's new neighbour. Eleanor's suite was right there too, across from Fern's.

It was something of a comfort to admire her own shady garden, the hostas blue-green and lush, the begonias full of blooms, her bleeding hearts shedding the last of their drops. Even from where she sat she could see a weed near a budding columbine and could hardly wait to get her hands on it. She wanted to kneel down, to dig, aware of nothing more than the pleasantly bitter smell of dandelion milk, the satisfaction of pulling something noxious up by the roots.

Olivia and Thelma had joined Eleanor and Fern and the four were seated already when a still-enthusiastic Mrs. Brown escorted the two men into the dining hall, her pantsuit seeming to trail an aqua aura. She introduced them to the people seated near the doorway, then settled them on the other side of the room.

"So, that's him." Olivia stared blatantly for a moment.

"Yes," Eleanor said. Eston seemed reticent and ordinary, although with his stooped posture, wattled neck and bushy eyebrows he struck her as resembling a cartoon vulture. But he didn't look capable of kicking a dog, let alone the crimes his daughter's book accused him of.

Olivia straightened her back, her plump face with its incipient dewlaps taking on an expression left over from her days organizing rallies for the CCF. "His life should contain nothing but misery," she said. Her British accent was always clearer, more clipped, when she was angry.

Thelma seemed more excited than distressed. "Now that he's actually here, we can start making plans."

Eleanor took in Thelma's heavily made-up face and scrawny neck, which right now she'd like to wring. If it weren't for her and her meddlesome daughter, they'd all be eating a nice roast beef dinner in blissful ignorance, mildly distracted by the arrival of a new resident.

"Oh, Thelma." Fern simply looked depressed.

Eleanor noticed Andrew Stuart watching her, his spare figure outlined against the doorway. She avoided his eyes. She wished, desperately, that she could go for an evening out with him again with nothing more to worry about than a foolish desire for romance. She should at least nod at him, let him know she'd see him later. But by the time she looked up, he'd disappeared. Maybe the menu today didn't appeal to him. Or maybe he saw how preoccupied she was, involved as usual with the women from her book club.

After dinner she stood at her living-room window looking bleakly at her garden plot. Without the other three to encourage or irritate her, the situation looked hopeless. She noted without caring that her bleeding hearts were drooping in the heat, and that the hostas looked parched. From now on, she was doomed to worry about Donald Eston. She and her friends would discuss nothing else, and he would monopolize her thoughts until something was finally done.

Abruptly, she went to her broom closet and grabbed the duster. She returned to her windowsill, flicking the fake feathers with too much energy, threatening the safety of her knickknacks. She slowed down. Her ornaments were mostly of glass, gifts of crystal vases and figurines her son and grandchildren had collected for her during their travels. Dusting them was usually a comfort to her. Her glass menagerie. She lifted the duster from the curves of the Costa Boda vase to admire the copper blue suffusing its clarity. She picked up the Swarovski jaguar from the shelf and held it to the light, polishing the arc of its back with her sleeve.

2

(Two Months Earlier)

Spring had blown abruptly as always into Saskatchewan, melting snow into slush one day, whirling dust over dandelions the next. Now the elms bordering the grounds of Pleasant Manor Seniors' Village displayed hard knots of buds revealing a hint of chartreuse, perennials pushed through to the light of days that lasted long enough to induce the seasonal amnesia Eleanor Sawchuck thought peculiar to her province. It wasn't as if the winter hadn't existed, but as if it were something so long in the past and far into the future it could be discounted. Having coffee near an open window in the lounge with Olivia and Fern, she relished the sunshine, looked forward to a walk in the fresh air, despite having to use a cane. She almost caught, wafting through the atmosphere, the scent of something like euphoria: Andrew Stuart had invited her out for a drink at the Legion. She smoothed her hair, glad she hadn't succumbed to a perm or dyed it away from its natural iron grey. She knew at her age she had no business being vain about her looks, but was aware that a version of her old prettiness still crossed her face now and then.

Then Thelma Johansson walked into the lounge, looking crabby. Not bad-tempered, but crab-like, with her big eyes half-hooded with age, her skinny legs, and the way she scuttled up to their table. She carried a plastic No-Name bag that seemed to contain only books, but she set it down as if it concealed an explosive device. "Corrine lent me the perfect book for our club," she announced, "now that we're supposed to be talking about evil."

Eleanor raised her eyebrows at Olivia, wanting to lift herself free of the light mire of doom Thelma could induce when she was in this sort of mood.

"Ah, really? The perfect book!" Olivia's expression took on a light scepticism. She reached under her dress to straighten a strap of her girdle. Olivia was a solid block of a woman always armoured in foundation garments under flowered dresses that should have looked old-fashioned, but somehow she'd retained the flair from her slender days for making anything she wore seem stylish.

"I'd like to buy a vowel," someone said on the TV which was set up on a raised platform where the altar used to be. The room held an odd mix of easy chairs, a couch, and various tables set up as if sprouting organically, changing places at the whim of the activity coordinator. Eleanor often wondered if the ghosts of the nuns who used to worship there were upset at the use made of their chapel, or if they thought, well it was better than having the old convent demolished altogether.

The lounge still featured a small stained-glass window portraying a stylized woman in luminous azure kneeling in front of a haloed, Byzantine-fashioned Christ, which Fern appeared to be absently examining. Her lips moved to follow her thoughts, her white candy-floss hair floating in airy filaments caught by the spring light. But she shrugged her narrow shoulders and turned to Thelma. "You're lucky your daughter shows such an interest," she said, her voice strong and sensible as usual.

"Yes," Olivia agreed. "None of my lot reads anything other than the odd thriller."

Thrillah. When Eleanor first got to know Olivia almost sixty — could it be sixty? — years ago, she'd sometimes found her own rs disappearing. A war bride, Olivia had kept the vestiges of an English accent and an odd colonial manner, commanding and genial at the same time.

"Corrine thinks the Last Chance Ladies' Book Club could do with some serious reading material," Thelma glanced pointedly at the plastic bag. Eleanor examined the vaulted ceiling of blond wooden beams on flaky white plaster that right now looked as if it were ready to start crumbling down on them. The little Christ in the stained-glass window, gazing heavenward, seemed to be rolling his eyes too.

Fern held her coffee carefully in an unsteady hand. "Our reading material has always been serious," she said. "Serious literature, at least."

"What kind of book is it, Thelma?" Eleanor asked. Not for the first time, she regretted showing nothing but passive assent when Thelma volunteered herself as the fourth member of their book club. Thelma considered anything non-fiction to be serious reading.

"This is a really powerful piece of non-fiction," Thelma said, and Eleanor let an impatient click of the tongue escape. Who did Thelma and her daughter think they were, to decide what was good for the four of them? She gazed at Thelma for a moment too long. Her hairdo, a puff of rusted steel wool, just suited her wiry frame and brassy personality. As usual, she wore too much makeup, with bright red lipstick that bled into the wrinkles of her upper lip.

Thelma ignored her. "It's about a girl horribly abused by her own father. A true story from her point of view as a child, really intense, portraying how she felt as it was happening. Terrible. You have no idea. When she grew up, she killed herself after writing the book as a sort of suicide note."

"Oh, come now." Shock mottled Olivia's face. "We want to enjoy ourselves here. Exercise our brain cells as we did with *Heart of Darkness*, not give each other nightmares."

"I'm not enthusiastic about reading that type of thing either, Thelma," Fern said, rather too mildly, Eleanor thought.

She assumed Thelma knew her opinion would be the same as that of the other two, but found herself automatically accepting the book as it was thrust into her hands. "Here," Thelma said. "It's a short read. Just take it home with you and have a look."

Eleanor pictured herself throwing it back at her but then thought, as usual when she was bullied by Thelma, this wasn't worth fighting about. She would put it away unread until Thelma forgot about it.

The book felt light in her hands, thin as a volume of poetry. The cover featured a view of a house with an outside wall missing, like a dollhouse, with the figure of a small girl curled up in a corner.

The menacing shadow of a man covered all the rooms. Verging on melodrama, she thought. The name of the book was *Many Rooms*, which, she read on the title page, came from the Bible quote beginning 'In my father's house.' "I can take it home," she said, "but that's no guarantee I'll read it."

Thelma held up the other copies like an auctioneer. "It's an impressive piece of writing as well as a riveting story," she told Fern and Olivia. They finally gave in, accepting their copies, but obviously thinking that they too would just put them away. "Once you start, you won't be able to put it down," Thelma predicted.

Eleanor's coffee didn't taste right; she thought maybe the milk had been sitting out too long. She decided to brew some fresh at home and said her goodbyes. As she walked out into the May sunshine, the book in her hands seemed to gain weight.

On a wet evening later that week, Eleanor took *Many Rooms* off her shelf. By now she was used to having it around, had looked at the cover and title page a number of times. It was, after all, only a book. She could quit reading whenever she wanted. She drew the blinds against the raindrops distorting the dark and sat in her armchair where the lamp was adjusted properly over her left shoulder, although she'd never understood why light from the left was best. After one last glance at the shadow of the man on the cover, she began to read.

She was immediately drawn into a first-person, visceral account of horror beginning when the girl was tiny. Repeated rapes. More appalling, almost incomprehensible abuse committed not only by her father, but by acquaintances who paid him, all this happening on an acreage near a town in Alberta. She read it right through, with a mix of ashamed fascination and abhorrence and finally a hatred so profound that when she finished reading, her lungs felt constricted, as if she'd never breathe properly again. She put the book down and sat in shocked stillness, watching the clock measure its slow time before she went to bed.

She dreamed the same dream in a repeating cycle throughout the night. She was walking down a street and saw the girl's father coming towards her, wearing a fedora and expensive topcoat. She attacked him over and over, with her bare hands. She awakened to an ash-coloured dawn with the feel of her fingers on his throat, his Adam's apple crushed by hands which were, in the dream, young and powerful.

With the furnace turned on because of continuing rain, the air in the lounge hung overheated and dense in spite of the high ceiling. By now, they'd all read the book. Olivia handed the plastic bag to Thelma, her mouth skewed in disgust as if she'd tasted it. "We certainly will not be using this as a discussion topic," she said. "I never want to see or hear of it again." She sat bolt upright on the lounge's worn leather couch. "Shameful," she went on, "the sense of fascination one feels reading this sort of thing."

"But seriously," Thelma said.

"Seriously!" Eleanor interrupted. Thelma glared at her, just for a second.

"That father," Fern said. "What did he see when he looked in the mirror? A man?"

Eleanor was reminded of a photo of a death camp she'd seen after the war. The expression of one of the guards. She had wondered the same thing. What did these men see when they looked at themselves?

"I think," Thelma said, "that such strong reactions show we should focus on this book and use it. We're discussing books about the nature of evil. Well, here's a prime example of pure evil if I ever saw one." She raised her pencilled eyebrows, making her seem almost youthfully excited.

Fern took a tremor-free drink of her coffee by supporting one hand with the other. "My God," she said, following her own thoughts rather than the conversation. "Each of those rooms. Used for something different." She was staring at her copy as if it had started to decompose right there on the coffee table.

Olivia nodded. "That's what I can't get over — the other men he sold her to by the hour. That father was lost, he was as much of a monster as someone like Idi Amin. But all those others! And this happened before everyone owned a computer. How would he *find* those men? Who would know…?" She was too mystified to finish the sentence. She took off her glasses to polish them with her cardigan.

Fern began to talk about her years teaching school, how over all that time she'd been able to pick out a number of her students who were obviously mistreated or neglected. In a few cases she'd gone to the school board but nothing was ever done. "And I didn't pursue it," she said, her voice shaking, elderly, her lined face looking even thinner than usual. "It never occurred to me any child could be going through even a fraction of something like this."

"All those men, from just the one area." Olivia couldn't seem to get beyond the paying customers. "And so many professionals. A doctor. A teacher. A *judge*, for God's sake."

"Don't forget the priest," Thelma added. "As if that's any big surprise." Eleanor could see how pleased Thelma was that they'd started a discussion in spite of themselves and decided she wouldn't say anything. But her friends' reactions were her own, the fascinated horror, the disgust, the simple bewilderment.

She recalled the years after her husband, Orest, came home from the war, when he had the nightmares he wouldn't talk about. His reticence must have been because of her, because she hadn't wanted to know. She always flinched from knowing details, from realizing the personal price paid by individual victims.

"Does education encourage perversion, somehow? Olivia asked. "Do educated men feel more entitled to indulge themselves?"

"No," Eleanor had to say, because she'd realized the only sensible answer. "It would all come down to cost. The working-class pervert wouldn't be able to afford any little trips out to that acreage. He'd be limited to what he could find at home."

Other people were starting to drift into the room so they finished their coffee and, to Thelma's obvious disappointment, decided to call it a day.

Thelma organized a meeting at her place.

"We haven't even decided on a new book to read," Eleanor objected when she phoned.

"But I have some news," Thelma said.

She greeted Eleanor at the door, pale and subdued, her face almost bare of makeup. "Come on in. Fern and Olivia just got here."

Had someone died? Had one of Thelma's several and far-flung children been in an accident? Ushered into the living room, Eleanor examined the familiar print of a storm-tossed sailboat hanging above Thelma's couch. She knew its twin, sailing in another direction, graced the beige wall by her head, and felt obscurely threatened.

The three of them weren't yet settled in with their coffee before Thelma came right to the point. "I've heard some troubling information from Corrine. Something she didn't mention earlier."

So, it was her youngest daughter, Eleanor thought. At least Corrine was within easy driving distance.

"Corrine? Is she ill?" Olivia asked.

Thelma hesitated. "That man from *Many Rooms*," she said bluntly. "That father?" She let another moment pass, whether from anxiety or a desire to prolong the suspense Eleanor couldn't tell.

"What about him?" Fern asked, annoyance shading her voice. She looked rather hawk-like when she was irritated.

"His name is Donald Eston. He's on a waiting list to get into Pleasant Manor." Thelma's skinny legs were crossed at the knee, one foot a nervous pendulum.

"What? Here?" Eleanor buttoned her sweater against a chill.

"Yes. That's why Corrine lent us the book. So we would know all about him, about this criminal moving in among us."

"Criminal!" Olivia levelled an admonishing eye on Thelma, the pink draining from her face in patches. "That implies a human being who's broken a law. This being is inhuman. Monstrous."

Fern stared at Thelma blindly. "Good lord," she whispered.

"He'll be here? In Pleasant Manor?" Eleanor couldn't take it in. "This isn't Corrine's idea of a sick joke, is it?"

Thelma didn't bother to reply. "He's been living in Crystal Creek, believe it or not. Less than an hour away," she added unnecessarily. "Been there for about five years."

Setting her mouth into the stiff upper lip of her heritage, Olivia said, "We'll have to do something about this."

"That's what I think," Thelma said.

Sick with apprehension, Eleanor noted Thelma's face had regained its colour, her voice its officious edge. "Do something?" Eleanor repeated. "What on earth can a few old women do about someone like him?"

"Remember, he's no spring chicken either," Thelma said. "How hard could it be for four women of our age and experience to make one man's life miserable?"

Eleanor closed her eyes for a moment. Was Thelma joking about this?

"It's obvious," Fern said. "We'll have to get rid of him."

"What exactly do you mean, 'get rid of'?" Olivia asked.

Fern gave her a look. Her tremor had almost disappeared and she was unusually focussed, tense with concentration. "I mean we should object to the authorities and keep him out of here."

"I don't think murder's all that bad an idea," Thelma said.

"What authorities?" Olivia asked, ignoring her. "The Pleasant Manor executive? They can't even manage to get rid of a leaky faucet."

"Corrine should have told us about him being on the waiting list." Eleanor said. "There's no way I would have read the book if I'd known the main character was going to show up in my own life."

"That's the very reason she didn't tell us," Thelma said. "She thought we couldn't know the full extent of his crimes unless we read about them. And after all, we were discussing books about evil. It seemed to her like fate dropping everything into place somehow."

Appalled, Eleanor remembered the dream she'd had after reading *Many Rooms*, the anger and disgust and the shame at her own fascination. Thelma was nervously playing with a coil of her hair, not looking at any of them, though Eleanor couldn't imagine that she'd have expected any of them to be happy with her daughter and this new information.

They sipped their coffee in a silence that soon grew ponderous. There was nothing more to say, Eleanor thought, until he actually arrived.

"Maybe in the end," Fern said, "he won't show up."

"Yes." Olivia brightened. The colour in her cheeks resurfaced in splotches, the way it had disappeared. "He might die. Or make other arrangements."

Thelma had recovered. She examined her cuticles as if, now that she'd told them about the man and his plan to move in, she had nothing worse to worry about than a hangnail. "We'll just have to wait and see," she said.

3

They agreed they had no choice. Now that Eston had appeared among them, they would have to do something. There was no use simply exposing his identity. Nobody in Pleasant Manor would have read his daughter's book, or would want to. People would gossip, but in the end, they'd come to the easiest conclusion: that Donald Eston had been wronged by an unstable, attention-seeking daughter. Because no one here, no one they knew, could possibly have done anything like that. And so the book club would be the ones labelled as troublemakers.

They rarely used the formal facilities offered by the Manor for club meetings, but somehow today it seemed appropriate to use the boardroom. The dainties provided by the kitchen sat untouched, the fat plops of chocolate haystacks, the bricks of Rice Krispie cake and rickety uncles all looking anything but dainty. The fluorescent lights intensified the plain white of the walls and reflected off the faux oak of the table. Eleanor had to breathe deeply to ease a tinge of nausea.

"Anyway," said Thelma, "we want to handle this on our own. Starting gossip like that would kill our anonymity." She was in full makeup today, ready for anything.

"If only we could assume it was all gossip," Olivia said. "If only we could ignore him." She seemed smaller today, or vaguer, Eleanor thought, less substantially there.

"What the hell was Corrine thinking?" Eleanor asked Thelma.

"I thought we'd given up blaming Corrine," Thelma said. "She just wanted us to know about him. For our own safety, if nothing else. Who knows what he's still capable of?"

Eleanor was angry partly because she hadn't seen Andrew for days now, had told him she wasn't feeling well, which was the truth. Trying to straighten her spine, she felt as if a last straw were settling on the back of her neck. She could not let this business ruin her life. Tomorrow morning she would let Andrew know she was feeling just fine.

Thelma said she'd been doing some research on the internet. "I was serious when I said murder wasn't a bad idea." Her eyes seemed particularly hooded today, Eleanor thought.

Nobody responded. Eleanor wasn't sure if Fern and Olivia were simply taken aback into silence as she was, or considering the possibility.

"Well, of course only as a last resort," Thelma acknowledged. "It may not be practical, anyway. But there are a number of common plants that are very poisonous. Monkshood, foxglove, castor bean. We could find those right in our neighbourhood. We could dry one of them, grind it to a powder and put it in a muffin or something."

"Right," Eleanor said. "And then all of us could present it to him. 'Here's a muffin our friend Thelma baked just for *you*.'" But when she saw that the other two seemed to be calmly ignoring Thelma's idea altogether, she regretted saying anything.

"Would Corrine have any ideas, I mean about what we could do, Thelma?" asked Fern. She wasn't shaking right then, but she looked wan, her wrinkles more pronounced, as if the effort to control her tremors enhanced them.

Thelma said she didn't really know. "She hasn't given me any suggestions." She sat back, examining them all with a baleful expression. She was disappointed, Eleanor thought. She'd looked forward to intrigue, to living in one of the crime novels she liked to read.

None of them was able to come up with anything other than ridiculous ideas for punishment ranging from cruel and silly practical jokes to harassing phone calls quoting lines from *Many Rooms*. There was not one thing Eleanor could picture herself actually carrying out.

"There is something," Thelma said. "Something simple that would do to start out with." She glanced at Eleanor. "Don't worry, it has nothing to do with poison." She hesitated, scrutinizing the blank boardroom wall.

"Well?" Eleanor asked.

"We could send him a note that says, 'We know who you are.' We could paste the words together from letters cut out of magazines. To make it seem more sinister, if nothing else."

Eleanor stifled any comment, but then thought, to hell with it. This didn't sound much better than anything else they'd come up with. "That seems a bit juvenile, doesn't it? Cutting and pasting a note together like a group of schoolgirls?"

"It might force him to think twice about wanting to stay here," Fern said, being charitable, Eleanor thought.

"I doubt he'd leave because of something like that," Olivia said. "But if by some chance he did, it would solve the problem. For us at least." She reached under her collar to adjust that perpetually loose strap, and Eleanor, vaguely irritated, wished she'd give up on foundation garments and buy a few empire-waist dresses, or stretchy pants and loose tops like everyone else.

"It would mean we did *something*," Thelma said, not looking at Eleanor. "And this would be only a first step. We'll just take this one little project at a time. The more I think about it, the more interested I've became in vengeance."

"God help us," Eleanor said. "But if you want, go ahead." She had no intention of doing any cutting and pasting herself. "Slip it under his door some night."

"I will," said Thelma. She looked around, her crimson lips pursed. "I'll just do it myself then. Any other suggestions?"

They gave up and called the meeting to an end. Olivia wrapped the dainties in paper napkins and handed them each a share.

Eleanor was walking up and down a hallway, exercising as usual, except she was holding onto the arm of her father-in-law, Maksim Sawchuck, who had died years ago. They walked at a steady pace. Donald Eston sat in an armchair by a window, and each time they passed him, Max would pause and wave and Eston would look up and smile. Eleanor could see he was masturbating, hiding his erection with a colourfully illustrated version of *Alice in Wonderland*. "Don't you see what he's doing?" she asked Max, who turned to her with a disdainful expression and said, with no trace of his Ukrainian accent, "Don't you see what you're doing?"

In the morning, shakily drinking coffee, she asked herself what the dream could have meant. She supposed it was obvious, father figures and sex: all that. She often dreamed about Max, though she never dreamed or even thought very much about her own father. Like Tom, her brother who'd become a drunk, her father had made her feel bereft long before he died. Diminished by the thirties, her father had lost his mettle, lost some element vital to his character that left him indifferent yet perpetually worried. She recalled her dad as a sort of ghost, sitting in one place for hours, staring off into an alternate universe.

Her mother, a pretty and lively woman, stocky and strong, had become the breadwinner. She took on what cleaning jobs were available in town, driving in with their old Model T and "doing" for the doctor and pharmacist. She cleaned the Catholic and Lutheran churches when they didn't have enough volunteers. She managed the livestock and a big garden. Eleanor's father pretended to farm, and her grown brother came and went, pretending to help out, stealing what money he could.

She saw her mother become old before she was well into her forties, and when Eleanor was thirteen, she had a nightmare about watching her mother dwindle into a doll-sized corpse. She remembered over breakfast the next morning saying, "Mom. I've decided to quit school after grade eight and find work."

"You're such a bookworm you'd finish high school with no problem, and that's what you're going to do," her mother said. "You can work for people during summer vacations." Her father hadn't even looked up from his coffee. He had long since given up having any say.

Max Sawchuck had been another kind of man altogether. Andrew, with that attractive intensity of his, reminded her of him. She'd been too young to have anything to do with Max. Too virtuous. Now, with Andrew, she was afraid she was simply too old.

When still a teenager but with four summers of employment under her belt, she'd worked one late summer and fall harvest as a hired girl for Max and his wife, Anna, who was still recovering from the difficult birth of her tenth child. Eleanor at seventeen considered Anna and her middle aged and shapeless body so different from herself they were like two different species. All those babies. Although aware her own mother's situation wasn't worth envying, she knew for a certainty Anna's kind of life would play no part at all in her own future.

But Max. She wasn't used to powerful men. He'd seemed immense to her then, compelling, his presence like a magnet. A magnate. That was how he behaved, more like an oil magnate than a Ukrainian immigrant farming a sandy half-section of land.

Orest had been there too, on leave from the army for a few days, and she'd noticed him, been flattered by his watching her. But compared with his expansive father he seemed colourless. Although he was taller than Max he seemed smaller, somehow, his nature cramped and cynical. She only later, after she'd been out dancing with him, saw this as thoughtful and knowing.

She'd slept on a cot in a tiny room with three of the youngest children, each of them round-headed and cheeky, like the kids in *The Little Rascals* movies. Whenever she ran into them later on, no matter how old they were, she saw their toddler selves. She had been so sleep-deprived that now she recalled those days as nothing but a fog of chores: barn and garden, canning, housework, baking and cooking for the threshing crew. How she had the energy to have a crush on Max she'd never know.

But the crush had been something real. She began to imagine nameless world crises in which everybody except her and Max evaporated in some painless way. Even when he was right there in front of her as she was serving him his meals or handing pails of chop over the rails of the pigpen, she'd think, what if the two of them were the only people left on earth. She began to arrange her hair attractively around her face instead of tying it back. Tightened the ties of her housedresses to show off her figure.

Then she came upon him one day washing up at the pump, his overall straps hanging from his waist. She was able to watch him up close and half-naked for several minutes as she held an empty pail, waiting her turn. Even now the memory was a gift. His shoulders. Those massive sheltering shoulders and the deep chest with a great T of black hair.

Her fantasies gained focus. When she found herself making actual plans, deciding to stay home from church so she could be alone with him, she frightened herself. She knew it was time to leave. She told the Sawchucks she had promised her mother she'd be back to help with the late fall canning, and besides, if she were going to graduate she'd better start attending school. Anna was feeling well by then anyway. She was able to do every one of her duties properly again, she assured Eleanor blandly.

Of course, Max must have sensed something. If he'd been a certain type of man, he could easily have taken advantage.

Then, after the war, Eleanor set out to win Max's son as if he were a school prize, and they were married. But no matter how content she was, wed to Orest, it took some time for Max to lose that indefinable magnetism. Well, of course it was by no means indefinable, but naturally she wanted it smothered if not dead and buried. She had to enter a certain state before she walked into his house, a cool shell that Orest's siblings took for snobbery, which meant that when they got together with his family for Ukrainian Christmases and Easters they were treated like guests. She sometimes wondered about Orest, what exactly he knew about her. He was as stubborn and thick-headed in his own way as his father, but he also contained a self-awareness that could have extended to her. She'd never liked to wonder what Anna did or didn't know.

Max had died of a cocktail of cancers, lung, prostate and liver, when he was seventy-five. He remained at home with Anna until his death, his daughters helping out, taking time from their jobs and families. Eleanor wanted to take her turn, although Irena said, "Mom doesn't expect you to; there's enough of us, Eleanor, though it's nice of you to offer." Even so, toward the end, she had insisted.

She and Anna were comfortable enough with each other by then. Over the years, Maksim's temperament had worn Anna down until she was like a stone polished by ocean waves: smooth, impassive. But while not normally talkative, Anna could discuss every one of her children and their offspring with the minute interest of a scientist examining life forms under a microscope. "That Dennis, he's a simple one, but scrape him deep he's a mystery," she might say. "And then you scrape furder, you get right to the middle of that heart of his and he's simple again."

Anna never talked about Max except to say once, "Maksim, he lost himself there in Banff, making those tennis courts for rich people."

"Yes," Eleanor said. "Three years off his young life. But then so did the men who went to war. I'd rather be flattening a tennis court in Banff than fighting in the trenches in France."

"Ah." Anna looked at her as if she were a child. "It was great shame and waste of his time, he never forgets. It made him homeless, so he don't ever feel part of this country."

During the First World War, Max had been sent to a forced labour camp, not in Germany but in Canada. Since Ukraine was then part of the Austro-Hungarian Empire, many Ukrainian Canadians had been rounded up, their rights taken away. Along with thousands of other Ukrainian men, Max was forced to help build the national park system. He'd been sent to work in Banff.

They were not systematically tortured or starved into hollow-eyed skeletons. But those trying to escape could be shot. They were imprisoned, living in tents winter and summer, forced to build roads and tennis courts and plant lawns for the Banff Springs Hotel. Years stolen from their lives. Max told Orest he'd intended to fight for his new country. Austria was no friend of Ukraine, but even if it had been, he would have done his duty. As it was, imprisoned as an enemy alien, he'd rather have broken rocks. What kind of legacy was it to make wild land comfortable for the rich, for *tourists*? He'd spat out the word, Orest said, like an obscenity. When the next war came, in spite of the farm exemption, Orest and two of his brothers went off to fight for Canada.

During Max's last illness, Eleanor was there against her common sense to let him know, to make him aware of her. What she needed was not absolution but confirmation. She had a compelling desire to say certain words to him out loud.

She had him to herself only an hour one afternoon, when Irena took Anna for a drive. "Just to get her out of the house," she told Eleanor. "God, she's been stuck here, she's stuck by him like a leech since he took ill, she'll make herself sick."

He was still able to sit up in bed, though he was becoming weaker every day. Anna had trimmed his moustache and he kept stroking it, rubbing the tips of his fingers over the stiff bristles that had replaced the sleekness he was used to.

"Ah. Eleanor." She brought him the herb tea that always followed Irena's visit with his shot of morphine. If Irena hadn't been a nurse it would have been far more difficult, maybe impossible, for him to die at home.

Supporting his head with each sip, Eleanor could tell he was comfortable once more. Stoned, as her son Dennis would have said, but his mind seemed relatively clear. "Max," she said. "I have a secret to tell you."

"A secret? What you want with secrets?" The pupils of his dark eyes had narrowed to pinpoints. Wisps of hair grew in tufts on his yellow skull like a half-grown chicken's feathers.

"When I was seventeen, I fell in love with you."

He looked confused. "With me? Seventeen? Hah." His face regained its focus. "You're teasing me."

"No. I'm telling you the truth. I was in love with you for a long time. With Orest too," she assured him. "But at first, it was you."

He was silent for a minute, then nodded, giving Eleanor the impression he'd recalled something he'd known a long time ago. "You were only a child." He closed his eyes, seemed to nap, but when he opened them again said, "With me? Hah." He laughed, but looked pleased this time rather than scornful, then settled back once more with his eyes closed. Soon before the hour was up, he opened his eyes and examined her keenly. "You're a good woman, Eleanor. And pretty, too. I always said so."

He said this lightly but he meant it, and she took it to heart. She was good. She was pretty. No matter how cynically she tried to put these terms into perspective, his praise had sparked a radiance that she could feel again now, remembering, though she knew even in Ukrainian he wouldn't have been more eloquent. He would not have said in any language that she was wonderful, lovely, that she'd enhanced his life by existing. He thought she was a good woman. That she was pretty. It was enough.

She did love Orest, certainly as well and eventually instead, simply because familiarity, along with contempt, hurt, and annoyance bred laughter, comfort, and affection. And there was of course the real sex, which as it happened was worth any amount of fantasy.

That morning in the lounge, when she saw Andrew sitting by himself she worked up the courage to bring her cup over to his table. "Do you mind some company?" She knew she was being forward. Neither of them was a morning person; they were not yet comfortable enough to sit in grumpy silence together.

But Andrew smiled at her, pleased. "Of course not! Sit down."

Set doon. She liked everything about him, his Scottish accent, his spare physique, his trim white sideburns. She even found his baldness fetching.

She stirred canned milk into her coffee. "I only want to let you know I feel better," she said. She sensed a table of women watching her from across the room. Annoyed, she turned her back on them and glanced over at her friends, who weren't paying her any attention at all. Thelma was on the alert for her own beau, Palmer Foote, who had just returned from visiting his son in Toronto. What Palmer saw in Thelma, Eleanor couldn't fathom.

"You certainly have been wrapped up with your book club lately," Andrew said.

Was he complaining? She found this somewhat gratifying, but on the other hand, he wasn't her — what did her grandchildren call their sweethearts? — partner. "The psychology of evil," she said, "hasn't turned out to be as much fun as we expected."

"Good," Andrew said. "Let's go out this evening, maybe to the Gem. We could go to the Legion later. Or" — he looked around the room in mock apprehension, as if he were going to suggest something wicked — "we could go to the beer parlour."

"Oh." She smiled. "I don't know about that."

In the end, all they did was meet in the lounge to watch a Sherlock Holmes special on PBS. The only people there that late in the evening, they sat side by side on the leather couch with a respectable distance between them, a gap she was far too conscious of. She tried to concentrate on the new Holmes: a very good likeness, really. Rather too much meat on his bones, but he had the right air, the right look about him. Eccentric, ruthlessly single-minded, ascetic.

Preoccupied with the program and with Andrew, Eleanor didn't look away from the TV until the station took a break to solicit funds. Glancing at the doorway, she gave a small cry of alarm, startled to see a child of seven or eight peeking into the room, a calm, curious expression on her pasty little face. She had the impression the girl was settled there, that she'd been scrutinizing them for quite some time.

"Well!" Andrew said genially. "And who are you, up this late on a school night?"

Discovered, the child sauntered into the lounge, clutching a cookie from the Manor kitchen. She was wearing a stiff new pair of jeans and a bright yellow T-shirt, but had a neglected, stubborn look. Eleanor would have wagered the backs of her ears weren't clean.

The child ignored Andrew and continued to look at Eleanor. "Have you seen my gramma?"

Eleanor found her voice. "Who is your grandma, dear?"

"Bea." The girl sat down comfortably. Her hair, Eleanor noticed, looked as if it contained a bit too much styling gel. Or no. It had recently been washed but the shampoo hadn't been rinsed out properly. "She's not my real gramma, she's even older than that. She's my great-gramma. I only just met her when we moved back here."

"She must mean Bea Armitage," Eleanor said to Andrew. She had an uncomfortable sense that the girl found her interesting, but only up to a point. The way a C student might scrutinize a germ under a microscope.

Bea Armitage was one of the few second-floor inhabitants allowed to roam the first-floor hallways at all hours, even though she had Alzheimer's, or something of the sort. The second floor harboured an infernal mix of the crippled and demented. The physically and mentally challenged, Eleanor corrected herself. She had been up there only once, on her orientation tour two years ago.

"Yes, that's her. Bea." The child now turned to examine Andrew.

Andrew grinned comfortably at her, as if kids appeared in the lounge on their own every day. "You can sit with us here and watch TV till your grandma shows up. She'll be in to fetch her budgie sooner or later."

Eleanor smothered a silly gleam of pleasure. How comfortably intimate that sounded in his accent: ye can sit wi' us here. "Has Bea shown you how Kilroy rides on her shoulder?" she asked. "Your grandma is his favourite person."

"I've seen that bird lots of times already." The child looked scornfully at Kilroy's cage hung beside the angel wing begonia in a corner of the room. The bird was eating, busily spreading seed shells around. He looked up for a moment, beadily examined the humans and produced a polite old lady cough, "Ahack-ahack," the only thing he'd ever learned to say. Andrew turned the TV to the kids' channel, to a cartoon featuring grotesque articulate toddlers. "*Rug Rats!*" The girl transferred her interest instantaneously, immersing herself in the television program as if this were her real environment.

With a sinking sense that she should do something, Eleanor decided she would have to find Mrs. Brown. Tell her to impress on the kid's mother that Bea wasn't fit to look after herself, let alone a new-found great-granddaughter.

But as if on call, Mrs. Brown walked into the room. "Chandra," she said to the girl, "your mom's waiting for you up in Grandma Bea's room."

"Tell her I'm watching cartoons," Chandra said.

Mrs. Brown raised her eyebrows at Eleanor. "All right. Your mom can come down to get you. Just be ready to go in five minutes." She nodded at Andrew and left. When Chandra's mother didn't appear, Eleanor walked the girl to the elevator. She rode up with her but sent her down the second-floor hallway alone, deciding she'd done enough.

She had the nightmare about strangling the father from *Many Rooms* again, and wondered why the man she attacked didn't look like Donald Eston. Maybe the dream, once imagined, would always remain the same.

But Donald Eston was there, a real person, living across from her. She could see him come and go, his bent form becoming familiar, although she never talked to him. He seemed able to straighten his back if he made an effort. He often stood taller to greet people politely, didn't seem secretive or particularly solitary but didn't attract acquaintances. He seemed a bit lonely. She saw nothing whatsoever about him to indicate the monstrous father in that book. Did his politeness look a bit too smooth? Did his habit of examining the ground he was walking on seem suspicious? Well, of course anyone with even a slight crook in his back would tend to look down.

Drifting preoccupied into the lounge next morning, she was annoyed to find Thelma alone at their table. Where were Fern and Olivia? She sat down, prepared to make conversation.

"It was easy," Thelma whispered.

"What was easy?" Eleanor knew she should be grateful Thelma didn't seem to be holding a grudge.

"I pushed a note under his door," Thelma said.

"No!" Eleanor relaxed into surprise. "You actually did it?"

The arrival of the other two interrupted them. "I know I look like The Wreck of the Hesperus," Fern said, her hands shaking more than usual, "but I've hardly slept a wink lately."

"Join the club," said Eleanor. She noticed Fern didn't help herself to coffee, and wondered if she should offer to pour her a cup. Instead she said, "Thelma put that note under Eston's door last night." Now that Thelma had done something, no matter how inane, she thought she should try to be encouraging.

Olivia seemed surprised but not disapproving. She sank into her chair slightly too fast, making it creak. She was about to say something when Megan, the new kitchen aide, came by to make more coffee and replenish the tray of dainties. She was already one of their favourites, sprightly and confident, with purple rinse in her hair and a new ring through her eyebrow. "Gee, you're all looking conspiratorial this morning."

After an instant's hesitation, Olivia said, "Thelma's heard some juicy gossip." She cleared her throat and looked benignly into Megan's eyes.

"Oh?" The girl waited, coffeepot raised.

Eleanor examined the floor tiles.

Thelma said casually, "It's way too awful for your young ears, dear." She patted the back of her permed hair.

The girl shook her head in mock disappointment. "You're just too bad, Thelma." She wandered over to the water tap.

"Harvey Cruickshank's girl," Fern said. "I just noticed the resemblance. I taught him in grade five."

"I think that little diamond chip in her nose looks rather sweet," said Olivia, "but a pierced *eyebrow*?"

"You're quick thinkers, both of you," Eleanor said to Thelma and Olivia. "I couldn't come up with a thing to say." They beamed at her, pleased with themselves. She was glad to be able to offer something positive, especially to Thelma. Today she was just tired of conflict.

They were almost ready to leave when Donald Eston walked in. Hunched over more than usual, he made his way through the obstacle course of tables until he found a seat to himself. Passing him on the way out, Eleanor sensed misery covering him in an almost visible blanket and she felt a sickness of heart. They walked silently down the hallway to the exit, none of them looking at each other.

Fern had convinced Murray, the caretaker, to paint one wall of her living room a dark sage colour. Eleanor approved. She thought it added style and a contemporary feel to the room. Along with Fern's modern grey couch and chair, the Lindner prints and aboriginal artwork she'd bought years ago from various galleries in Saskatoon, it looked like something out of *Western Living*. The four women were all there trying to relax with gin and tonic. None of them drank much any more, but each had a bottle or two of something she liked stored in her cupboard.

Fern opened a window and snapped off the screen to reach the window box of pansies that formed a mound of velvet blooms ranging in complexion from royal purple to violet. "I can't stand looking at these deadheads another minute." She pinched off the dried and drooping flowers. Noting Fern's baggy jeans and frayed sweatshirt, Eleanor wondered, not for the first time, why she couldn't transfer some of the care she expended on her home to herself. Even when she was young, once Fern finished her school day she would change into clothes only suitable for the ragbag, as far as Eleanor was concerned. She wore rolled-up jeans and patched lumberjack shirts long before they became fashionable in the fifties.

The smell of newly mown lawn filtered into the room. Eleanor heard a dog barking in the distance, a man speaking angrily nearby. She got up to join Fern at the window. "It's coming from Eston's place." The evening light had a hazy orange cast to it from a forest fire hundreds of miles away.

It was Eston's son, leaving. "Forget it, Dad. This is the end of the line here. I'm sick to death of you and this whole business." As he slammed the door, Eleanor could see his expression. She ducked behind Fern's sheer curtains. He drove away squealing his tires, escaping.

Disgust, she thought. He looked disgusted. Maybe he knew his father was guilty, even if he might not admit it to himself. Eleanor could imagine how it might be for him. How immediately after the book came out he would have denied any possibility of its truth, claiming his sister was mentally ill or vicious, her suicide evidence of both. But over the years, he would remember things in spite of himself and come to a state of repressed knowledge, an oily comprehension rising toward the surface when he was under stress. "We've been forgetting who this man is," Eleanor said.

"What we've been forgetting," Fern said and then stopped. "I started wondering after this morning. You know, we've never even considered the possibility of his innocence. That book was so convincing, we've taken it all along as gospel."

"I know it's true," said Olivia, "even if all the facts aren't." The gin and tonic had made her even more flushed than usual, but she sounded coolly sure of herself.

"Oh, Fern." Eleanor knew the book was true, had felt it in her bones when she read it. "No one could possibly make all that up. Not with such depth, such believable detail."

"That's what I thought too." Fern absently fingered one of her diamond earrings. Not normally someone who wore jewellery, she'd bought them for herself when she turned sixty and never took them off. "But now I'm just not sure. A talented writer can be very convincing."

"I don't know if I told you this," Thelma said, her eyes hooded, her rouge showing in irregular circles because she'd turned pale. "Corrine said all the neighbours suspected something, but of course everybody minded their own business. No one said anything until after the book came out. Now if we talk ourselves into considering him innocent, we'll be almost as culpable as they were. We'll just be avoiding responsibility."

"Responsibility?" Eleanor asked. She could not let Thelma get away with thinking her stupid note was a responsible action. "The only thing we've done so far is play one mean trick."

The truth was, no matter how she felt about the father in that book, the thought of punishing a flesh-and-blood Donald Eston had become almost inconceivable. She simply didn't have the stomach for vengeance on someone else's behalf. Like herself, Eston looked to be a quiet, reserved person, sociable enough to play the odd game of cards, show up in the lounge for scheduled entertainment. He seemed like a human being.

"I guess when it comes right down to it," Olivia said, "we're stymied. Maybe the only answer is to call in Corrine, see if she can come up with anything."

Thelma said they should just make themselves do something. Hire an assassin. Put ground glass in his oatmeal. Trip him in the hallway.

"Maybe we should be careful," Eleanor said. "He's certain to try to find out who sent him the note."

"Yes." Fern rubbed her forehead as if she had a headache. "If he's the kind of person he's accused of being, maybe we should be afraid of him."

Eleanor knew Dennis had seen her at the window watching him get out of the car with Beth, because he walked in without knocking. He gave her a brusque hug and said, with no preliminaries, "You've got to let me bring you that TV, Mom. It's just gathering dust in our guest room."

Eleanor shook her head at him. This was an old argument. If she had a TV, she would waste half her time staring at it like an old lady. "I'm not about to have my peace and quiet invaded by the idiot box, just so you don't get bored waiting for me when you drop by and I'm not here," she said.

"Mom. You have to put on your jacket and walk all the way over to the Manor just to watch the damn news." She was about to remind him she had a perfectly good radio and that Fern had a TV, but just as abruptly as he'd brought the subject up he let it drop. He wandered over to her small fridge and stood holding the door open, contemplating the contents until he finally grabbed a container of yogurt. "Mmm. Blueberry. My favourite." Eleanor was beginning to wonder when her son would show signs of taking over and becoming the parent as, theoretically, he was supposed to. She glanced at the yogurt, then at Dennis's stomach and lifted her eyebrows.

Her daughter-in-law was still outside on the steps, examining the window box. "Your begonias are blooming really well this year."

"Yes," Eleanor said. "They're twice as big as last year's." Beth finally came in, taking off her sweater, a zippered sweatshirt with a hood. Eleanor tried to ignore a prick of annoyance. Beth loved clothes; she dressed to the nines for work every week day, but putting on something halfway decent to visit her mother-in-law never seemed to cross her mind.

"I can't get over how you've made this every bit as neat and comfortable as your old house. Hasn't she?" Beth asked Dennis, looking around as if his mother had accomplished a miracle. Whenever she visited, she seemed to focus on how well Eleanor had settled into Pleasant Manor. Not for the first time, Eleanor suspected that after her fall Dennis had considered inviting her to live with them. She knew Beth had been right to say no, but still, it would be gratifying to have been asked.

"Beth. You've been saying that now for two years. Mom's getting tired of it."

"People never get tired of having their housekeeping praised." Eleanor said this before she recalled she'd never had the urge to praise Beth's.

Tall and thin with greying blonde hair, Beth reminded her of Fern. Besides having similar builds and colouring, they both had that schoolteacher bearing, a wary vigilance that, after years of being directed at students, extended outside the classroom. She and Beth should have known each other better by now, but Eleanor had become resigned to, even appreciated, carefulness. She'd certainly never become chums with her own mother-in-law. She had a sudden recollection of herself having a few too many drinks with the neighbours after a curling bonspiel. "Dese robber boods," she'd imitated Anna. "Dey don't lasted longer dan one darn pair of socks." The memory made her blush, jabbing her with shame fifty years too late. "I'll make some fresh coffee," she said.

Beth made a move to help but Eleanor waved her away from the tiny kitchen area. "You two sit down and relax."

"I hear you're having some interesting discussions in your book club," Dennis called from his usual place on her chesterfield.

"What?"

"Your book club. Mrs. Ostenyck told me you were reading stuff about the nature of evil."

"Good lord," Eleanor said. "How would she know?" Ursula Ostenyck wasn't even that much of a gossip.

"I guess there's not much going on around here that people don't talk about, eh?" Beth said sympathetically.

As Eleanor took out the milk and sugar, she wondered if anyone had the gall to gossip to Dennis or Beth about her and Andrew.

Now that her book club had been mentioned, it occurred to her she could tell Dennis and Beth about Donald Eston. Thelma wasn't the only person with offspring who might be able to come up with some suggestions. But she should ask the others first. Then she thought, what the hell, they wouldn't object, they were desperate. They'd all be grateful for advice from anyone with a new perspective.

After they'd helped themselves to coffee, but before she could reconsider, she said, "Can you two keep a secret?" She sat down on her green armchair across from the couch.

Dennis rolled his eyes and blew into his cup. "Of course." Beth nodded, perking up.

Eleanor smiled grimly. They thought they were in for some gossip, likely about Thelma and Palmer Foote.

She told them about *Many Rooms*, about what Corrine had found out, about that father being here, now. Living right in Pleasant Manor.

"His daughter lived alone for years in Edmonton. Corrine said she had a job shelving books in a small branch library. Then she wrote *Many Rooms*, and just after it came out, committed suicide."

Both of them looked stunned. This wasn't anywhere near what they'd been expecting.

Dennis looked away. "I don't know, Mom. Thelma is sometimes a bit off the wall, you said so yourself, and her daughter likely isn't far behind. Where did she get hold of this book, anyway?"

"It's been out for some time," Eleanor said. "Since the eighties."

"Well, then…" he hesitated. "How could something like that have gone on without someone knowing? Or doing anything about it?" He finally looked at her. "It must have, I mean the police would have investigated something like that when it all came out. They must have found there was no evidence."

"I don't think she ever laid formal charges," Eleanor said, "and the book's publisher had to say it was fiction. But it's understood to be a memoir of actual abuse."

"If the girl is dead now," Dennis went on, "you can't do anything for her. And as for doing something to the father, I can't think of what, if the police haven't charged him. They can't kick him out of Pleasant Manor for being a character in a novel."

Eleanor expected Beth to be more sympathetic, but her expression too looked closed, careful. The lines around her eyes and mouth, Eleanor noticed, were becoming wrinkles. "Remember that town outside of Saskatoon," Beth asked, "where all those people in that daycare were accused of having horrible rituals? And then it turned out to be made up, by one disturbed kid?" She tapped a fingernail against her cup in a nervous rhythm. "Ever since that all came out, I've considered this sort of story with a grain of salt. Think of those lives, all those innocent adults whose lives were ruined."

"That's right," said Dennis. "If the proper authorities haven't seen fit to look into it after the book's been published and out there for twenty-some years, why should you and your Last Chance Ladies think you have to do anything?"

Beth gave Dennis a quick look. "Eleanor, I think sometimes you and your club wind each other up about things. I mean," she hesitated, but forged on, "if the guy hasn't even been charged, let alone found guilty, I just don't know."

"She killed herself," Eleanor said. "That has to mean something. In effect, her father murdered her."

Dennis sighed and looked down. He glanced back at Beth but didn't say anything.

"So really," Eleanor asked them, "your advice is to mind our own business and forget about him?"

"I don't have any advice, Mom." Dennis now sounded annoyed. "I just know we have enough problems of our own, and so do you."

She looked at her bad knee and nodded. "You're right about that, at least." A heavy disappointment lodged in Eleanor's chest, not just with Dennis and Beth, but with humanity in general. And with her herself, at a creeping relief at being granted permission not to care.

"This must be really upsetting for all of you," Beth said. "I think Dennis and I should think about it for a while, maybe find someone to talk to."

"I'd like to have a little talk with that Corrine," Dennis said.

"I'd rather you didn't," Eleanor told him.

Eleanor thought she had become used to pain, thought of it as playing a minor melody to the rhythm of her life. She didn't realize how much better she'd been feeling lately until her knee flared up again. But pain or not, she had promised herself never to vary her exercise routine. Besides her scheduled therapy, she continued to walk every day. If she let herself get away without making the effort, even once or twice, she was sure she'd begin a slippery slope of self-indulgence that would lead to certain knee surgery. She was afraid of going under the knife. Not that surgery was difficult to avoid in Saskatchewan. She'd been on the list, just in case, ever since her fall over two years ago, and had yet to be notified even to confirm they knew she existed.

This morning she was going for her walk inside the Manor. She never walked outdoors unless Fern was with her, or Andrew. If she went outside alone, she feared she'd stumble, or go a bit too far and find herself stranded. After a sleepless night she felt as if she were the only person left on earth, or on some other godforsaken planet, struggling in a limbo of white walls and bare windows that looked out on an iron-blue sky. Could you call limbo godforsaken? She knew she was wallowing in self-pity, and so what. Looking down at the ugly green tile polished to a high hospital sheen, she noticed a hair preserved in floor wax. Now it would irk her every time she passed it. Glancing at her rubber-soled shoes, she recalled a pair of high heels she'd once owned, lovely black patent leather with ankle straps. In those shoes she'd danced with soldiers, the rough wool of their khaki jackets brushing her breasts, their hands hot against her waist. Max Sawchuck's son was one of those soldiers, the only one able to dance as if he were the source of the music. She fell in love with Orest at one of those dances.

Eleanor caught a glimpse of something cloudy out of the corner of her eye. It hovered there for a split second, making her turn her head as if she'd heard a sound. This had happened before. She knew it was a trick of vision, likely brought on by the shiny floor or the windows lining the wall. Maybe it was only the sides of her glasses, or maybe she was developing cataracts and would have to have surgery like Olivia. But this time when she turned to look she did see something there. A grey silk scarf had been left, fluttering on a coat hook over an air vent. She reached instinctively to finger the material, and with no warning she was there on her wedding night, for a split second felt the glide of her nightgown as Orest undressed her, the silk catching on his calloused hands.

Oh lord, that whole first year of marriage. In the spring while working in the garden the simple act of bending over to pull dandelions could steep her in longing. She would hear the distant noise of the tractor become louder and immediately be overcome, damp and weak with knowing Orest couldn't stand to wait any longer either, that he'd unhitched the rod-weeder and was making a special quick trip, wasting gas just to see her. He would thunder into the yard, come to her black with summerfallow and she didn't care, his hands diving under her blouse to cup her breasts until she sank into the grass, and now she remembered how hard he was against her skin, the smell of earth, grass, garden weeds, caragana. The smell of him.

Bea Armitage came by, the budgie clutching her shoulder, and Eleanor took a deep breath, relieved at the distraction. Bea stopped, and in an instant had grabbed the scarf. "This is mine," she said, slyly as a five-year-old. Eleanor nodded and looked away. She was in no mood to get involved with the ins and outs of Bea's mind. It was a shame, really; such a waste. Bea was so healthy otherwise, strong and slender with skin stretched tightly over good cheekbones. The words "Higher State" stood out on the front of her dusty-rose sweatshirt. The budgie clucked and chortled, nibbling her earlobe.

"Gramma Bea!" A child's voice called from the far end of the long hallway. "I'm going to the lounge. Spongo Bob's on." Chandra looked a bit healthier, Eleanor thought. She had some colour in her cheeks, likely because she'd been eating meals at the Manor. She showed up regularly now, always with Bea in tow for the first half hour or so. It was as if Chandra were the one babysitting. Bea seemed to consider the child a puzzling but unavoidable appendage, even though Chandra always ended up watching TV in the lounge with Bea roaming the hallways as usual. When it was time to go home, the girl would just leave.

A touch of sickness, the slight nausea that could become an actual pain at the top of her stomach, began to bother Eleanor as she walked on. That child had weighed on her from the first. Chandra. What kind of name was that? Maybe she could convince Olivia to have a talk with her mother. If anyone could have an effect on the care of that little girl, Olivia could. But then again, Thelma said the mother was an alcoholic. Eleanor knew from years-ago bitter experience with her brother, Tom, that a good talking-to would come to nothing. She headed for the door, suddenly deciding she could very well walk outside alone. She felt desperate to be out in the open, hoped that fresh air would clear the rubble from her mind.

Tom was an old grief, one that she'd put away in anger years ago. He'd drunk himself to death by the time he was forty-five and caused so much misery to everyone around him that forty-five hadn't been early enough, as far as she was concerned.

Her parents had died while Eleanor was in her thirties. Her mother wasted away with cancer, reminding Eleanor bitterly of her nightmare about the doll-sized corpse when she was thirteen. After her mother's death, her father lost what little will he had to live. He died of exposure one night in winter, supposedly out looking for a lost animal. But Eleanor always suspected that he'd gone for a walk and, tired of life, simply lain down in the snow.

Tom had sometimes been threatening when he was drunk, but Orest was able to handle him. It was his perpetual whining between benders, his wheedling and lying and stealing that Eleanor found so sickening. She recalled finally ending contact for good when, on one visit while asking to borrow money, he'd had the gall to pocket one of her few ornaments. She saw him do it. It was a glass owl her little son had bought for her at Woolworths in P. A., worth nothing to anyone but Eleanor. When she confronted him, he was convincing as always. "Eleanor." He said this in the mildly critical way he had when she was a little girl, when he was her beloved and bold older brother. "What would I want with any of your trinkets?" After Tom died, Eleanor and Orest buried him next to her parents. She regretted that. She didn't like picturing Tom perpetually nearby, somehow continuing to grieve them.

She had a nightmare again, nothing to do with Eston, but about a miscarriage, a baby she'd lost a couple of years before she had Dennis. She dreamed the child had somehow survived, was now a little girl growing up without her, and that Tom was taking care of her. She woke up in an agony of worry.

5

Eleanor glanced over at Andrew, admiring the way he used his cane as if it were a stage prop rather than a real one. Her friendship with Andrew was continuing without, she thought, making much progress. When she'd first come to Pleasant Manor, she'd resented having to associate so much with the opposite sex. Hated having to be aware every single day, in spite of her age, of the impression she made as a woman. When Andrew arrived, she tried to think of him as he was: an old friend of her husband's. But even then, his moving there had added colour to her life, a tinge of vividness to the pastel monochrome that was taking over her days in Pleasant Manor. Now that she had other worries, he provided distraction.

Thelma had been having an open affair with Palmer Foote for over a year and didn't seem to care about the gossip, the sly ridicule that Eleanor knew she and Andrew would find intolerable. But Palmer wasn't as shy as Andrew. He would come right over, interrupt their morning coffee to commandeer Thelma, his broad face beaming on all of them, not caring how annoying they might find him. "I'd like to be a fly on the wall at one of your women's lib meetings, there," he'd said just a few days ago. "Lord knows what you four are plotting."

"Women's lib meetings?" Olivia looked at him as though he'd suggested they were learning how to skydive.

"Oh, he's just trying to get a rise out of us," Thelma said. "Come on, Palmer, I could use a bit of exercise." Eleanor remembered thinking that Thelma didn't need rouge when he was around. Thelma had walked purposefully toward the door, her slim figure disappearing in front of Palmer's bulk as he followed her out.

Eleanor told herself she should be happy that Andrew continued to invite her for walks like this, viewing gardens around the neighbourhood. She stopped to admire Barb Felbert's tiger lilies. Their vigorous orange spikes dominated the Felberts' back garden.

"So how are your book club meetings getting on?" Andrew asked. He referred to the club carefully, Eleanor noticed. "Have you found a new topic yet?"

"Not since we gave up on the psychology of evil," she told him.

He produced a small snort, and she wanted to give him a tap on the arm as she used to when Orest made fun of her. She made do with giving him a look, and he grinned. She pictured herself reaching up, kissing him right out there in broad daylight. Why not? But of course she didn't do it. Because it was up to him. She'd always left that sort of thing to the man, hoping he'd pick up on her unspoken invitation. Of course, that was a lifetime ago.

When Andrew had started paying attention to her, she began to recall old romances, nights with young boyfriends that were more vivid than whole years of her marriage. Or whole hours she'd spent yesterday. She was starting to recall her youth in a golden glow, she thought. Like a senior citizen. She could easily bring back the enjoyment of being kissed, of allowing a certain amount of fondling. She recalled Frank Laliberty after he joined the army, trying to convince her it was her patriotic duty to make love with him. "I may be killed in action," he'd said, flushed and desperate. "Do you understand what I'm saying? In a few months from now I might be dead."

"Frank." She'd sat up, knocking her elbow on the steering wheel. "That's just blackmail. It doesn't put me in the mood for anything, it only makes me mad." She made him drive her home, and he was killed within a year. There was no golden glow to that memory. All those boys, dealing with death and horror. How old had he been? All of nineteen.

"Andrew, how did you hurt your leg?" She asked the question before considering.

He stopped for a moment, adjusting his grip on his cane. "Well, you know I was shot in the war. Thigh damaged, muscles and tendons gone to hell. It's not a pretty sight, but at the time I was thankful not to lose it."

Any fool could see what the results were. She wanted to know how it had happened, the circumstances. But she lost the nerve to push for an answer. Orest had never talked about the war either.

Andrew was watching her now and she looked away, self-conscious. He had a piercing gaze that seemed to become stronger each time she saw him. She wasn't sure if it was directed at her specifically or at the world in general, but it made her weak in the knees. Well, not weak, exactly. And not her knees, exactly. She looked down at her bad knee, annoyed with herself.

She was sure Andrew liked her, but because he was so circumspect she couldn't be certain of his intentions, if they were romantic or not. What an old-fashioned phrase, she thought. Romantic intentions. But really, she didn't know. More than likely he wanted companionship with an old friend. Which was, of course, all she should want, too.

She used to know when a man was attracted to her. Now she'd lost that easy knowing, along with confidence in her own sex appeal. But of course, at her age, what did she expect? What did she think would happen? Sex? She'd had no one since Orest. She glanced at Andrew and brushed away the thought of a stupid joke Thelma had told her.

Had she ever really had any confidence? She'd known when she was young that she was pretty enough, sweet-faced and curvaceous, with creamy skin. She would sometimes turn in front of her wavy bedroom mirror half in love with her own body.

What was Thelma's joke? Something about an old woman from Kentucky and KY jelly. Good lord.

"Considering you don't have a new topic," Andrew said, "you and your friends seem to be having some serious talks there."

"I suppose we are." Her absentmindedness didn't seem to bother him. He was a tolerant man, she thought. Wise. "We've got ourselves tied up in some disagreements about evil," she said, "and we can't seem to come up with anything to replace it." She had at one time considered telling him everything, all about Donald Eston. He'd lived a life, after all, he would have an opinion. But she didn't want to involve him in something so ugly. She wanted to keep him aside, as someone representing a part of her life that held nothing but pleasantness.

"How about the nature of truth?" He looked away, then right back at her. "Or love?"

Her mind went nearly blank. "Oh, we're sick of trying to be philosophers." She smiled. "We need to go back to concentrating more on the books themselves. When our topic was Sex in Victorian Literature we had a great time talking about books like *Wuthering Heights* and *The Old Curiosity Shop.*" She stopped, unexpectedly embarrassed.

He grinned, sure of himself again, and she made a little face at him. Self-conscious for flirting, wondering in fact what her little face looked like now, she pretended to admire another garden they were passing. Caragana leaves glowed emerald, delphiniums added the blue missing from a silver sky.

The back alley led to the Kinsmen playground and an aging but still serviceable set of metal and plastic swings, teeter-totters and a climbing apparatus. A gang of children was playing tag, zooming around in a group as well-coordinated as a flock of birds in flight. They were running with sticks, and Eleanor repressed an urge to call out to them to be careful. One of them climbed the monkey bars with his weapon in his mouth like a pirate and stood balancing at the top, waving at them. Andrew waved back. "It's our little friend," he said.

"What friend?"

"That girl. Remember? Bea Armitage's granddaughter?"

"Oh! Chandra." Eleanor waved too. Squinting, she could see now that the child wore girl's running shoes and her hair was cut in a short shag. Her stomach gave a familiar twinge. "Someone's going to put an eye out," she said, "running so fast with those sticks."

Andrew grinned at her, and instead of continuing around the block, steered her farther on, toward the new blacktop on Main Street. "We might as well go for coffee now that we've got this far," he said.

"Yes," she agreed. As they walked, she realized her knee felt so good she hadn't been conscious of it for some time.

Eleanor confided in Olivia, wanting to know what she thought Andrew's intentions were. "If you ask me, you should put yourself out more," Olivia said. "Make an effort to encourage him. Look at Thelma and Palmer, what a good time they're having." Her smile took on an unusual, rather sly look. "Take my word for it. In the end, sex is always worth it."

Eleanor laughed, a bit too loudly. Olivia's late husband, Zack, had always seemed not prissy exactly, but, well, the perfect United Church minister. Which of course was what he had been.

"You know, Eleanor, I'm not, I mean my life hasn't been perfect."

"No!" Eleanor laughed again, then saw that Olivia was about to tell her something important. "What do you mean?" She waited.

"I wasn't always faithful to Zack. Believe it or not." Olivia said this abruptly, her face blotching red. She spoke with that wheeziness, that slight whistle of the lungs that seemed common in fat people after any exertion, although she was just sitting there.

"Olivia!" Eleanor was shocked. "Really?"

"I've prayed for forgiveness, but the truth is I've never felt guilty."

"Really?" Eleanor heard her own voice rise to a squeak, but it was all she could come up with.

When Olivia fell silent, Eleanor finally said, "Well, you can't just not tell me now."

"Remember when we lived in Mont Herbert, and Harvey Malloy was the head of the church committee?" Olivia sat up straighter in her armchair. "He used to meet with Zack once a week at our house, Thursday afternoons at one o'clock, and after that Zack went on his hospital rounds until supper, spreading spiritual comfort to the ill, that sort of thing. It always took up the entire afternoon. Harvey would stay for coffee and cake with me. He was a widower, and of course by then our kids were gone, we were both well on into middle age."

Harvey Malloy. The name summoned a faint image of a bald, rangy farmer.

"It started with entirely innocent intentions, I always had baking and as far as I knew, he never got cake unless he was visiting someone.

And then one thing led to another." She was regaining her composure. "Thursday afternoons for two years, until we were transferred back here."

Eleanor couldn't quite believe what she was hearing. "And there were no complications? He didn't want you to, oh, I don't know." A tiny bone of resentment lodged in her throat, and she wondered why Olivia had never told her about this before. "Harvey Malloy," she said. She tried a matter-of-fact tone. "I think I remember him." She remembered Olivia, too, at the age she was in Mont Herbert. Fifty or so, beginning to gain weight. She'd always been pretty, with strawberry blonde hair and a peaches-and-cream complexion that aged well into her sixties. In fact, Eleanor realized, she'd looked a little like her own mother, but where Eleanor's mother was stocky, Olivia had been voluptuous. "Harvey. He died a few years ago, didn't he?"

"Yes." Olivia replaced a loose hairpin in her grey French roll. "I went to the funeral. Got Luke to drive me. I think the relatives were all rather mystified."

Eleanor imagined Olivia entering the chapel and sitting in a back pew like some mistress in a made-for-TV movie. "You mean you *hope* they were mystified."

"We enjoyed ourselves," Olivia said. "And no one ever found out. We were discreet, and never saw each other outside of those afternoons. We had cake too," she said. "Most afternoons we'd start out by sitting there, pretending to eat and chat, tantalizing each other. Saying things. It wasn't necessary to spend so much actual time in bed that way."

"Olivia!" Eleanor began to shake with laughter. She became breathless, her eyes streaming, her limbs finally so weak she almost fell over on the couch.

Looking a bit offended, Olivia waited for her to recover. "Everyone has secrets," she said.

6

Eleanor and her friends continued to keep a surreptitious watch over Donald Eston. Today they were all eating Sunday dinner in the dining room. On weekends the Manor was full of visitors, with various grandchildren running around like half-trained chimpanzees, but Eston always seemed impassive, indifferent. There were times now when Eleanor's interest in him was cool, impersonal, the idea of his existence and what it meant to society a riddle to ponder. Here was a human being, sitting right there in full view, who'd been capable of committing horrors. Or had he? And if so, what about now? Was he still a danger? Or did he recall his crimes as youthful indiscretions, his daughter as collateral damage? She wondered if he sensed them watching him.

"Of course, he might be especially wary after having received Thelma's note," Olivia said.

"Yes." Fern held her teacup with both hands. "That may have been a mistake."

Eleanor noticed that although at first Olivia and Fern were willing to refer to the note as 'ours,' lately, since nothing had come of it, it had become exclusively Thelma's.

"At least one of us did something," Thelma said. She raised her pencilled eyebrows, challenging. "Rather than being a mistake, it's likely made him think twice about actually trying anything." She stopped talking as Bea Armitage glided past their table, Kilroy on her outstretched hand pecking at her fingernails. Today she was wearing a mauve T-shirt that exactly suited her silver-white hair. Did she choose her own clothes, Eleanor wondered? Or did the aides on the second floor take pleasure in putting outfits together, dressing an elderly

Barbie? Then to her horror, Bea headed straight for Donald Eston, and when he nodded and smiled at her, she sat down. The two of them were soon in animated conversation, admiring the bird.

"Looks like Bea has made a friend," Thelma said, deadpan.

Olivia was uncharacteristically speechless. Fern stopped picking at a stain she'd noticed on her shirt and suggested maybe they'd known each other before.

"Not likely," Thelma said. "Bea is from Prince Albert. One of her sons lived here. Sid Armitage? Chandra's grandfather. Now him and his wife are both dead. Cancer, within two years of each other. Brooke's living there alone with Chandra, in their old house."

"Brooke?" How did Thelma know all this?

"Chandra's mother. Palmer's niece Nancy used to know her." Thelma had already informed them Chandra's mother had a reputation for booze and drugs.

Eleanor watched Eston hand Bea a butter tart. Bea ate the tart with delicate good manners, then stood up quickly and left the room, the bird now clinging to a napkin on her shoulder. Eston left soon after in his usual nondescript way, only slightly hunched over, his expression bland.

Bea had the mind of a child, Eleanor thought. Maybe she was the one he was interested in. But really she knew better.

"It's time to do something," Olivia said. "Now that he may be targetting a specific child, I think we should confront him."

Eleanor didn't like this idea, but could think of no alternative.

"All of us together," Olivia said. "Knock on his door and say, 'We've read your daughter's book and it seems powerfully believable to us. If you have anything to say, say it; otherwise just be aware, we'll be watching.'"

"Who knows who else he's abused?" said Thelma. "Or is still capable of abusing."

Fern was whispering to herself. With such a precise, common sense way of thinking, how Fern always managed to give an impression of befuddlement was beyond Eleanor. "We still have to consider…" Fern hesitated, then went on. "The plain fact is, his being nice to someone who's eighty years old is not a sign of guilt."

Olivia lowered her voice. "Fern. His sort of perversion is a physical thing. A physical attraction to young bodies. Not young minds. He's not interested in Bea. It's Chandra he's got his eye on."

Eleanor watched a hyperactive four-year-old run out into the hallway and disappear. Even if Chandra were never to show up again, some of these other children were here nearly every Sunday. No one looked out for them, least of all their parents. But she still wasn't ready to face down Donald Eston. Because who could tell what he'd do? And on top of that, to say right out that they would take responsibility, watching out for every kid that crossed his path…no. That would be insane. So she had to concede to Thelma. "After your note he already knows he has to be careful," she said. "It would be better to warn some of the other residents here instead. Tell them and say right out, we can't prove it's true, but keep an eye on your visitors."

"If we begin to spread this around, not only will people resent us," Fern said, "but they won't believe it. And Donald Eston will be certain to find out who did the talking."

They sat for a while in defeated silence. But they all knew they now had to do something, if only to find help. "Thelma," Eleanor finally said. "You have to invite Corrine for a meeting. She started it all. We need some advice here."

Thelma agreed.

Andrew had been dining with a friend on the other side of the room. Now Eleanor saw him standing near the entrance talking to someone she didn't know, glancing over at her, looking like an awkward boy baffled by a group of girls with secrets. A thorn of anger produced the now-familiar pain somewhere between her stomach and her heart. She was going to lose her chance with Andrew, and probably gain an ulcer. She was sick and tired of Donald Eston; she'd had enough. Why should she be forced into this preoccupation with something so unsavoury, so ugly, when she still had a life to lead?

Thelma was absentmindedly putting too much sugar in her coffee. "We had a long talk," she announced. She took a tentative sip, leaving a red imprint on the rim of the cup.

"Who?" Eleanor asked. She was distracted too, thinking again about Andrew.

"Corrine. Who else did we decide I should call?"

Eleanor saw Fern and Olivia exchange brief glances. She examined the ceiling, noticing a water stain that looked like Italy. That was the trouble with old buildings, she thought. They always had plumbing problems.

"The upshot was," Thelma continued, "Corrine wants to take us on an outing and then meet with us about Eston at the end of the day, and I suggested the Crystal Creek Sports Day. I used to enjoy baseball." She nodded toward Eleanor, glancing at the other two. "And you've talked about how Orest used to play and all of you went to his games. There's a pancake breakfast at the Legion Hall and so on."

No one said anything for a minute. "I don't know." Fern glanced at Eleanor and Olivia, her expression strained. "I just thought Corrine could come up with some ideas and run them past us. Doesn't she belong to some kind of women's group herself? She could ask them what they think we should do."

"Corrine can come and meet with us," Eleanor said, "but I don't know about her doing us any more favours."

"She never considered how strongly we'd feel about the situation," Thelma said, "how badly we'd be affected."

"She didn't consider us at all," Eleanor said.

"I think I'd rather enjoy a morning out," Olivia said carefully. She shifted a bit uncomfortably in her chair, making it creak. "I've been feeling tired lately, but a live old-fashioned baseball game might be just what I need."

Eleanor saw that Olivia was taking the high road. Why not, she thought, and decided to join her. "I have to admit," she said, "that I wouldn't mind seeing a game once more." Fern reluctantly agreed to go too, if only so that she wouldn't be left behind.

7

Thelma was pacing the sidewalk by the front driveway. Eleanor wanted to tell her that, for heaven's sake, Corrine wasn't even late yet, but held her tongue. When an activity was her idea Thelma was always a bit anxious and abrasive, sanding down a layer of the enjoyment.

But it was, Eleanor had to admit, perfect weather for a sports day. The Manor lawn gave off a new-mown scent. A robin flitted past; a magpie croaked boldly, pecking at a fast-food wrapper lodged among the petunias. Oblivious to Thelma's unease, Fern and Olivia had planted themselves on a wrought-iron bench, their faces turned towards the sun like morning glories. Olivia was looking particularly well turned-out today, Eleanor thought, in a new shift, a cool cotton creation with a pattern of strawberries on a cream-coloured background. Like Eleanor, Fern and Thelma wore casual stretchy pants and long blouses.

Corrine drove up right on time and slightly too fast, grinding to an abrupt halt in the driveway. "Hello, ladies," she said pleasantly as she hugged her mother. "Hop in." She swept her hand toward her car as if it were a royal carriage. She had a good figure for her age, shown off well in a black T-shirt and blue jeans, her hair tied back in a ponytail that looked too young for her. She had Thelma's big eyes, which right now revealed an awkward effort behind her cheerfulness.

"Hop in?" Thelma repeated. "Really, Corrine." She patted her rusty perm as if Corrine's hug had mussed it up.

Fern, Thelma and Eleanor insisted, as if there were any choice in the matter, that Olivia sit in the front while they wedged themselves into the back.

"We do appreciate this, Corrine," Fern said stiffly. "It can get expensive relying on the taxi." Eleanor noticed she'd dabbed on some pink lipstick for the occasion, a tad crookedly.

"Yes. And if we book the Manor van, we have to put up with anybody else who wants to come along," Thelma said, more enthusiastically.

Eleanor didn't have anything to add.

"I'm glad you could all make it," said Corrine after a moment. Her face registered nothing but a pleasant blandness. Nothing would be said, at least not right now, about Donald Eston or his daughter's book.

Eleanor, crowded between Thelma and Fern, thought that as parent of the host, Thelma should have been the one to sit squished in the middle. But as Corrine navigated the potholes and stretches of gravel on the highway to Crystal Creek, Eleanor relaxed. The August air was dry and invigorating. Crops of wheat and barley flaunted gold and olive-green heads not quite ready for swathing. The sky glowed blue, willows shone dusty silver in the pastures. Spruce and birch trees changed to bluffs of poplars as they neared the small town. Fern trained her bird-watching binoculars unsteadily out the window whenever she noticed anything of interest. "Did you know," she said, "that you can't tell when a bird is sick until it's on its last legs? They act healthy even when they're not, so the other birds won't kick them out of the flock."

"No kidding?" Thelma said.

"I'm starving," Olivia announced. Since they were planning to go to the pancake breakfast, they'd had only coffee and a bite of toast.

"Have you kept up your discussion group?" Corrine asked, as if she'd been waiting for them to break the silence. "Are you finding new books on the psychology of evil?"

"No," Eleanor said. "We haven't been talking much about books at all lately."

"Don't you belong to a group too?" Olivia asked amicably.

"Yes." Corrine's shoulders relaxed. "We get together once a month or so and discuss women's issues."

"And what sort of topics do you discuss?" Olivia asked.

"Oh, just about everything, nothing formal, really. Stuff to do with equality. We act on things too, we don't just talk."

Eleanor examined the back of Corrine's head. She'd better not be lecturing.

"Huh." Thelma laughed. "They started out twenty years ago with activities like examining their private parts in mirrors. They'd sit around without their pants, peering at little hand mirrors."

"Mom. We did that once. Once, and you never got over it. I still don't know how you even found out."

"I suggested they call themselves The Women's Action Team, and they were considering it until they realized what the initials spelled."

Eleanor was startled into a snort of laughter. Olivia gave an uncharacteristic guffaw, and Fern grinned. Corrine took on a long-suffering attitude. "We're activists who try to change things."

Crystal Creek's main street was somewhat narrower than Kasokinaw's, but otherwise pretty much the same except that its grain elevator hadn't been demolished yet. It still loomed, empty and derelict, over the railway tracks. One of Orest's brothers used to live in Crystal Creek, but Eleanor hadn't been there in years. A newly modernized drugstore shone beside the cracked stucco of the three-storey hotel, which hadn't had guests other than the occasional duck hunter for decades. It survived, like other small-town hotels, because of the beverage room on the main floor. A newer brick post office perched at the end of a row of old buildings with false fronts. Some of these had the weathered boards of structures waiting to be destroyed, some had been renovated into relatively smart little shops, some were simply kept up as well as waning finances allowed. The Legion Hall was on the outskirts, beside the baseball diamonds. Miraculously, Corrine found a parking space right by the front entrance. "This must be handicapped parking," Thelma objected.

"Well," said Olivia, opening the car door, "if the shoe fits." Eleanor hoisted herself out of the back seat behind Thelma. Fern was having trouble opening her door.

"Here, I'll get it from the outside." Corrine was infinitely patient.

Inside, the hall was crowded with people. Olivia, Fern and Eleanor found seats and held two while Corrine and Thelma loaded trays with plates of pancakes and sausages. "My, what a handsome young man,"

Olivia observed, watching one of the volunteer cooks flipping pancakes in a muscle shirt.

"You'd better be careful around handsome men." Eleanor grinned, thinking of Harvey, and Olivia frowned. Eleanor cleared her throat apologetically and gazed off into space, not wanting Olivia to regret telling her secrets.

They dug into their food with gusto. Crowds of families had turned out for a breakfast hosted by their favourite weatherman from Prince Albert, live. Entertainment was provided by a local country and western band whose lead singer had bleached and permed her hair so many times it reminded Eleanor of a stook of barley. Happily, this brittleness wasn't reflected in the quality of her voice. The band launched into "Queen of Denial" with such energy that part of the audience clapped and sang along. Kids crawled under the long plywood tables and played tag in the crowd. The hall didn't have air conditioning, but Eleanor never minded heat, especially now she was older.

Filing outside with the crowd, she had to stop for a moment behind Olivia, blinded by the light. The late morning air seemed incandescent, the sky bluer than sky blue.

The strawberries on Olivia's dress looked edible, glowing an almost luminous red. The huge wraparound sunglasses she'd worn ever since her cataract surgery gave her the air of an otherworldly star travelling incognito. Eleanor searched in her purse for her own sunglasses. "You look spectacular," Eleanor told her, feeling dowdy.

"I feel very good today. I'm positive I can even keep up with Thelma."

Out on the patchy grass the sun was toasting people in their shorts and T-shirts, its brightness reflecting off the hall's new white paint job. They strolled leisurely toward the ball diamonds, still following the crowd. Another band was setting up outside on a makeshift stage on the grounds where the hospital used to be; various kinds of races were being organized for the kids; a nearby slough sparkled in the sun. Red-winged blackbirds warbled their liquid calls among the cattails, mallards dipped and bobbed as serene as decoys in spite of the sports-day mob of humans only a few dozen yards away.

They climbed to the midsection of the bleachers, too high, as far as Eleanor was concerned. But she was still in an amiable mood, not willing to complain. She ascended with good grace, holding onto Corrine's elbow. The game began, with the Crystal Creek Raiders playing the Kasokinaw Kaycees. The grass on the infield was flattened almost as low as the dirt paths between the bases. The players punched their gloves. The shortstop spit. The umpire yelled something completely unintelligible that must have meant "Play ball!"

Eleanor was caught up, remembering the excitement of watching Orest pitch: the keenness of his concentration, his eyes narrowing, his whole self bent on zipping the ball past the batter. This pitcher couldn't hold a candle to Orest. He had none of his intensity, he was too conscious of the way he looked up on the mound. Overly relaxed, cool, he threw the baseball as if it didn't matter, as if it were only a game. The batter hit a grounder past second base, producing an unfamiliar sound, false and metallic. Ponk.

"Aluminum bats," Fern said, disgusted.

"Come on, Kaycees," Olivia and Thelma yelled, their elderly voices wavering past a group of Crystal Creek fans. One of them, a farmer in his forties, turned around and asked Olivia if her boyfriend was playing for the Kaycees.

"Clyde Peterson, any more of that and I'll have you writing lines," Fern called down to him. For a split second, Eleanor wondered if she'd gone round the bend, then realized that of course he was one of Fern's old students.

"Miss Albany!" He stood up, blocking a friend's view, grinning sheepishly. "How are you?" His friend gave him a good-natured punch and he sat down.

By the end of the game, the wooden benches had taken their toll. Eleanor's back hurt more than her knee. Fern said she was feeling a bit dizzy, Thelma had a stiff neck, and Olivia said she felt breathless. Corrine went to get the car, saying she'd drive it right up to the baseball diamond. Eleanor felt like one of a row of pigeons perched on an eavestrough as the rest of the crowd clambered down the bleacher stairs, some heading toward the other ball game still in progress, others gravitating toward the old hospital grounds to listen to the band.

She fingered her cane nervously, not looking forward to the climb down. She hoped Fern wasn't about to lose her balance, but she looked fine, serenely watching the wildlife in the slough through her binoculars. Still, Eleanor thought they should have insisted on sitting right at the bottom, should have asked some young people to move. Those teenagers harassing the defeated Kaycees, for example. She watched several shaggy-headed youngsters jostle each other as they walked off the field, teasing the ball players, their pants worn low enough to feature their boxer shorts.

"What a lovely morning we've had," said Fern.

Olivia was fanning herself, breathing heavily. "I just might take your advice, Eleanor, and get rid of my girdle. I could buy a nice empire waist next time we go to P.A." With no other warning, her breathing became a harsh inward bark. Before any of them had time to react, she fell against Fern.

Eleanor sat paralyzed, until she realized Fern and Thelma were struggling to keep Olivia from falling to the ground. She grabbed Olivia's arm and managed to help lay her on her side. Fern was shaking badly. All this was happening in a silence that seemed to slow everything down. Two teenage heads floated up from under the stands, and Thelma yelled at them to get help. After gawking in horrified indecision, they ran off, rearranging themselves on the way, the girl buttoning her shirt, the boy checking his fly. They hailed a van containing three men in baseball uniforms who drove up in time to meet Corrine, and they managed to carry Olivia down the bleachers and into the van. There was no use calling an ambulance; the nearest hospital was forty-five minutes away. Thelma took charge as Corrine was about to get in. "Corrine. You have to drive these two, I'll go with Olivia." Eleanor was too shocked and bewildered to object, though she knew it should have been she or Fern riding with Olivia on her last trip to Prince Albert, not Thelma.

She watched the van head out, horn blaring, and started to breathe in harsh sobs. The feel of Olivia's lifeless arm had remained in the palms of her hands, in her fingers, which seemed to have known there was no

Olivia there to grasp before she herself was fully aware of it. "It won't matter how long it takes to get there," she said.

"I know." Fern made her way back to the bleachers. Eleanor followed her, aware now of the ground under her feet. She realized she must have climbed down by herself, but couldn't remember doing so. A group of women appeared, hovering with concern and solace and paper cups of water from the hotdog stand. Eleanor steadied Fern's hands for her while she drank. Corrine, silent with distress, helped them to the car and they started off for the city.

Thelma met them in the waiting room of the hospital, her face drawn with grief. "It's all over. She passed away right there. At least she didn't suffer." She led Fern and Eleanor to a piece of vinyl and metal shaped like a couch and settled herself across from them in a chair that made a deep sighing sound as she sat down. "Luke is with her." Thelma had phoned the nearest of Olivia's sons from a cell phone in the van, and he'd arrived at the hospital before they did.

Corrine hovered awkwardly for a moment, then went off to make a phone call.

"We should never have gone anywhere," Fern said. She was weeping quietly.

Eleanor held onto Fern's arm as if she were afraid of drifting away and stared blindly at the padded chair beside Thelma, her eyes focusing only when Corrine joined them. "I can drive you home now, if that's okay," she said. "I'm so sorry."

"*This* wasn't your fault," said Eleanor.

"No. I mean I'm sorry for your loss."

"Oh. Yes, of course."

At Pleasant Manor, Mrs. Brown was waiting for them, ready with tea and condolences. Eleanor realized everyone within a hundred-mile radius knew about Olivia by now. They sat dazed and miserable in the lounge. Palmer and Andrew came in with rum to add to their tea, and their peculiarly masculine and uncomfortable solace. After sitting rigidly silent beside Thelma for several minutes, Palmer said, "We'll surely miss her."

"More rum?" Andrew had been silent as well. Eleanor shook her head no, although the first shot had warmed, encouraged her blood to flow again. She was afraid if she drank another one, she wouldn't be able to stop. She didn't want to make herself sick on top of everything else. And here was Andrew, making an obvious effort in front of all the gossips, just for her.

A number of people came over to express their shock and sympathy, and Eleanor felt grateful to them. Bea Armitage looked through the doorway and said, "I listened to the news. It's bad," and continued her walking. Eleanor wasn't sure if she was referring to Olivia or the news in general, but then Bea returned to the lounge, bringing the budgie over to them. "Have I ever shown you what Kilroy can do?"

"Yes, Bea, I believe you have," Fern said. She was holding one hand still by clutching it with the other.

"No, I haven't." She looked around to make sure no one else was watching. "This is our secret." With a sly look, she encouraged Kilroy to peck at her thumbnail. He trilled and twittered, fluffing his turquoise feathers so he looked twice his size. Then, his tail feathers fanning frantically sideways, he started humping her knuckles.

"For Pete's sake." Thelma was amused.

Bea smiled. Kilroy's eyes had become demented-looking, his black irises shrunk to pinpoints in circles of grey. He spread his wings over her hand, coming to a climax in a noisy cascade of liquid warbles. Abruptly, he was finished and quiet, his feathers sedately tucked in. He climbed up to Bea's shoulder and coughed discreetly in her ear. Bea whispered to Eleanor, "That's why he likes me the best."

The three women decided to go over to Thelma's for some peace and quiet and to glean some last comfort from each other before going to bed.

On the way there, Eleanor noticed Fern stop in surprise and look down at her purse. Her hands were clutching a white leather strap instead of her usual beige one. "I have Olivia's purse!"

"Where's yours?" Eleanor asked.

"Oh, damn it. I must have left it at the baseball diamond. Or in Corrine's car." She held up the roomy, shapeless leather bag as if she were auctioning it off. "I grabbed this when she started to fall, and then that's all I can remember. Maybe I should give it to Mrs. Brown."

"You can do that tomorrow," Thelma told her.

"The hospital must have needed her health card, though."

"I don't know what for," Eleanor said. "Can you get into your place? Were your keys in your purse?"

"I can get into Olivia's; she has my extra key. Had."

"Yes," Eleanor said. "She has mine too." Among the three of them, Olivia was the best at keeping track of small important objects. Eleanor touched the reassuring outline of her own key in her pocket. She remembered, when the book club had still been discussing Victorian literature, talking about the significance of keys in *Wuthering Heights*.

"I'll phone Corrine to check her car," Thelma said. "She should be home by now."

They stopped at Olivia's door, and Fern reached in the bag, then hesitated. "Maybe I should just go back to the Manor, get a key for my place, get rid of the purse." When neither of the others moved, Fern unlocked the door.

It was as neat as usual, but a window leading onto a box of pink geraniums was open, and there was a used coffee cup and toast-crumbed saucer on the kitchenette table. Eleanor half expected Olivia to call from her bedroom, "I'll be there in a jiffy. Make yourselves at home."

She stood there, shocked into stillness with the knowledge that this was likely the last time she'd see Olivia's apple-green-and-dusty rose living room. Though all the carpets and walls were neutral beiges and creams, Olivia had bought wall hangings, pictures, cushions and chairs to match her flowered chesterfield. Everything must have been at least five years old, but it all looked new. On a blond wooden table beside a pink African violet perched all her family graduation and wedding pictures, including Olivia herself looking slim and voluptuous in a satin gown and cat's eye glasses, Zack smart and upright in a double-breasted suit.

Olivia had looked like that picture when Eleanor and Fern first got to know her. Even back then, they used to go shopping in Prince Albert together, though none of them had much money. Fern always drove since, being single, she had a car to herself. Eleanor recalled that she and Olivia felt, not guilty but indulged, that there was always a sense that Zack and Orest had consented to let them have a day of fun without them. As plenty of husbands back then wouldn't have, Eleanor reminded herself. After Orest died and Eleanor moved to Prince Albert, Fern and Olivia used to drive in to visit her.

She remembered how the three of them would spend entire afternoons over lunch talking about everything from hairstyles to Dickens novels. They'd make bad jokes and laugh themselves teary-eyed. They'd gossip. They'd have such a good time that people would watch them, envious. She had a sharp recollection of Olivia ushering her and Fern out of a shop twenty years ago. "There's no use," she said, "in considering clothes that don't make us look better than we already do, which you have to admit, ladies, is pretty darn good."

Eleanor began to weep. Thelma washed and dried the cup and saucer. Fern closed the window.

The funeral was that Saturday, in the United Church. Corrine accompanied them, looking very nice, Eleanor thought, dressed in a light blue linen skirt and jacket and even wearing makeup.

"In Saskatoon she wears black whenever she goes out anywhere," Thelma muttered aside as they hovered near the church entrance. "Of course now that we're attending a *funeral*…"

"I can hear you plain as day, Mom, in case you think you're whispering," Corrine commented.

The three of them were wearing good dark outfits they'd bought when funerals started to become regular occasions. Olivia had owned a lovely suit of soft grey with a raised pattern of black velvet leaves. Eleanor wondered what would become of it now. The idea of that suit adorning a wire hanger in the Salvation Army was too depressing to contemplate.

Corrine had brought Fern's purse with her when she came to pick them up for the funeral, and Fern was concerned that she hadn't had time to change it for her black one. She looked ill at ease in a grey skirt and black jacket that was slightly too big.

"It looks fine," Eleanor assured her, "and who's going to notice, anyway?"

"Just about everyone," Fern said. She examined it. "Not that it matters." Eleanor recalled Fern often being concerned about what she wore teaching, never finding the perfect outfit that was both acceptably professional and comfortable enough.

After they found a pew, Eleanor watched Corrine settle in and realized that under her makeup she looked washed out and miserable. She felt a passing sense of satisfaction.

Considering the trickle of visitors Olivia used to have, the number of people who showed up for her funeral was astounding. An unfamiliar young minister mounted the pulpit, preening in his soap opera handsomeness, obviously looking forward to his own performance. He stood stalwartly self-conscious in his formal purple and white robes, flicking his black hair off his forehead. Once he started speaking in platitudes, it was clear that although he might have met her, he had no more of an idea about Olivia than he had about any other elderly lady in any community in the country.

"I've never seen him before, have you?" Eleanor asked Fern.

"He was Amanda's idea," Fern said. "He was her pastor in Saskatoon before she moved to Hamilton." Eleanor leaned forward to get a look at Amanda in the front row. Wearing an old-fashioned hippie-ish dress, she was now built like Olivia, though Eleanor remembered her as being quite svelte only a few years ago. When she was a skinny little girl, her eating habits had been one of Olivia's main worries.

Instead of accompanying the congregation, the preacher performed the hymns himself in his lovely tenor. Instead of praying for Olivia's soul, he prayed for a long list of troubled souls of the world.

As she followed the prayer Eleanor realized that, along with hungry children and people traumatized by war, she'd just prayed for "individuals with low self-esteem." Struck by a sort of psychic nausea, she raised her head, but by the time he brought out a drum to accompany himself in "Lord of the Dance," she decided she was too disheartened for anything but sadness. When the pastor graciously invited the congregation of mourners to sing along, she did, belting out the grotesque words and sprightly tune until she was choked with sorrow. She thought of Olivia, laughing, laying down Scrabble tiles for a triple-word score. She thought of Olivia, having cake and eating it.

8

Sitting outside alone, on a hidden bench behind the lilac bushes on the Manor grounds, Eleanor wondered if she would ever get over Olivia's death. She was so old, they were all so old, death should be no surprise, but it was just as hard to take as ever. She heard someone shuffling through the grass around the corner of the hedge and turned to see Donald Eston. He looked in poor shape, bent almost double. He stopped and for a split second looked taken aback, but then said, "I am sorry, Eleanor, for your grief." He gazed over her head.

"Thank you," she said.

He made his way back around the corner, his spine causing him obvious pain.

Fern came to sit with her, and together they watched dusk fall. "Donald Eston spoke to me," Eleanor told her.

"What did he say?"

"He extended his sympathies. He seemed genuinely kind."

Fern looked down at her hands. "The world is a terrible place," she said.

Intending to exercise for an hour, Eleanor found she was still tired out by sadness, although several weeks had passed since the funeral. She drifted toward the lounge after only twenty minutes of walking and found Thelma there, playing with the budgie. Kilroy was perched on her finger, puffing out his throat feathers and producing his polite little cough. "You see?" Thelma asked, as if she were making a long-argued point. "When Bea isn't around, he can be friendly with anyone. I'm trying to make him say 'Kilroy was here.'"

"Huh. You don't want him to become too friendly, Thelma."

Thelma laughed. Eleanor knew that in spite of their differences, Thelma had always wanted her to be warmer, less parsimonious with her friendship. And even before Olivia's death Eleanor had begun to appreciate Thelma's pluck, envied her willingness to have an open affair with Palmer. She wished she were half as brave and forward. In spite of telling herself she wanted only companionship with Andrew, she knew she was missing out, missing a last chance. She recalled the day Olivia had shocked her with the revelation about her affair with Harvey Malloy, telling her that sex was always worth it. She wished some of Thelma's nerve would rub off on her, some of her gregarious energy and indifference to gossip.

Besides, Eleanor was sorry for Thelma now, since it was because of her and her daughter that they'd all been under such stress. If she were Thelma, she'd feel guilty. She'd wonder if Olivia's heart attack had been caused by all the worry about Donald Eston. For that matter, she couldn't understand why she didn't hate Thelma, didn't blame her. She supposed it was because Thelma missed Olivia too; her grief was real. And, of course, it wasn't Corrine and Thelma's fault that Donald Eston existed. Finally, it wasn't as if Eleanor had many friends, or even knew many people who took a friendly interest in her. She'd better start appreciating those who were still around. "A hopeless case," Thelma said, shaking her head at Kilroy. "He'll never say anything."

Eleanor put her hand up to Thelma's and Kilroy hopped onto it to peck at her fingernails. She was surprised at how warm his little bird feet were. So close up, the budgie impressed her with his beauty. His body glowed turquoise, his wings and head feathers were a soft black and grey striped with yellow. His rather smug little face was yellow, his throat spotted with a purple necklace, and his long tail feathers flashed a startling indigo. "Hopeless case," she said to him, "hopeless case." Two perfect round seeds dropped as gifts from his beak.

Over coffee in the Gem Café, Eleanor was telling Andrew a funny story about Tommy Douglas, when abruptly, with no warning, she felt tears on her cheeks. The tears were just there, coming as easily as if she were some actress in a movie. "We should go," she said. She struggled out of the booth, apologizing. "I don't know what's wrong with me."

"Of course." Andrew left the coffee money on the table. Eleanor was glad the café was empty now. The waitress pretended to be intent on polishing the counter.

Eleanor could still remember when the booths featured red vinyl and Arborite with stainless steel jukebox menus attached to the walls. There used to be red geraniums in the front window. That was when Mrs. Yee was alive. Now oak-veneered booths contained benches covered in greyish-pink fabric and there was a row of snake plants at the front window. Even those changes had been there for decades.

Andrew led her outside and they headed away from Main Street, down one of the alleys of backyard gardens, where pansies and snapdragons were giving one last kick at the can before the first hard September frost. "It hasn't been long since Olivia passed away," Andrew said. "Realization is still sinking in."

She tried to smile. "I guess what set me off is that she was the one who told me that story. Of course Olivia and Zack knew Tommy Douglas, they were so active in the CCF." They headed towards Pleasant Manor, Eleanor now and then having to wipe her eyes. She thought of those windshield wipers you could set to come on intermittently.

"Tell me the rest of it," Andrew said, taking her arm. "So Douglas was saying? It was just after the war, he was marrying a newly decommissioned soldier and his girl?"

"Yes, well. It's just dumb, really. Olivia told it so much better. She could imitate him so well." She found a fresh Kleenex and blew her nose. "So Tommy said he'd finished the ceremony, and when he announced, 'You may now salute the bride,' of course…" she glanced at Andrew who was already smiling, anticipating the punch line. They were heading down the Manor's wide front sidewalk now, ready to turn toward Eleanor's suite, where he'd drop her off. She looked up at a sky of cotton-batting clouds scattered on blue ceramic. Her mind returned to the picture of the young soldier saluting his bride and she was weakened by a fit of laughter. She couldn't go any farther and stopped to give Andrew a little salute, infecting him too, so that they stood there hanging onto each other. Cackling like ninnies right in front of anyone who might be looking out the Manor windows,

When they finally struggled on, she realized Andrew was steering her toward his place. "Come in for coffee," he said. "You didn't finish yours downtown."

Her head seemed to contain a bee buzzing unhindered from one side of her skull to the other. "Okay," she said. They walked up to his door, which he opened before she could think straight. It was only after she was already half inside that she noticed several people out and about: Ursula Ostenyck watering her flowers, Lena Bole sitting on a chair by her front door, knitting. Henry Chance walked right by them and nodded. She thought if she backed out now it would seem very awkward. "Just for a few minutes," she said.

Inside his apartment, she sat down at the table. "I don't really want any more coffee," she said. The kitchen area was familiar, not only because it was much like hers but because she'd been there once or twice with Palmer and Thelma, waiting for Andrew to go out with them to the Legion. Everything was clean if not neat. Of course, he had the cleaning service in twice a month. An archway just like hers framed his living room, featuring a couch and chair from the seventies made of nubbly indestructible material in glossy burnt orange. A computer was set up on a desk by the window. "I'd better go. Did you see all the people around? It's as if they conspired to show up just as I came in." She stood up.

"Yes," he said. "I know what you mean; I'll walk you home." He was standing over her, very close. His voice had a rough sexy edge to it; his gaze focussed on her and she couldn't, didn't want to, move.

She looked up at him and he kissed her. They kissed for quite some time. She was astonished at how quickly lust could take hold. If it hadn't been for the sound of Lena Bole having a coughing fit a few doors down, she would have happily accompanied him to the bedroom. But she drew away. "Oh my," she said.

"Aye. Yes." He grinned at her, teasing now.

His mouth tasted like spearmint; he must have planned this. A quiet exasperation mixed with her euphoria as they headed outside to walk the gauntlet to her fourplex.

Eleanor and Andrew were now socially acknowledged as a dating couple. Several nights a week, they played hearts with Thelma and Palmer in the lounge. Fern sometimes joined them for coffee, but Olivia's death seemed to have destroyed something in her, a certain firmness of mind. She rarely came out to walk with Eleanor anymore, generally keeping to herself in her own place unless her friends insisted she come out, even if only to watch a movie with them in the lounge.

Now when she walked the hallway alone, Eleanor sometimes found herself having imaginary conversations with Olivia, telling her what was happening in her life, discussing theories and ideas, asking her opinion and coming up with what she thought Olivia would answer. She told Olivia how devastated Fern was by her death, that she thought Fern had always been a bit in love with her. Olivia would likely tell her not to be silly, but then she'd go on to say that love was complicated.

Today she was walking a bit later than usual because she intended to eat Sunday dinner at the Manor. She was hungry, and felt off, dispirited. She asked Olivia if she thought Fern appreciated her going on about Andrew. If Fern was depressed, maybe she didn't need to have someone else's happiness flaunted in front of her. Olivia would disagree, she thought. Olivia might say that listening to Eleanor's anxieties about sex and gossip would cheer Fern up, if anything. Eleanor decided to insist that Fern go for a walk with her before all the leaves had fallen, although the only garden flowers left now were a few sheltered asters and chrysanthemums.

The thought of fall flowers reminded her of the time of year she left the Sawchucks' farm, left before she could try anything with Max. Today that fall seemed clearer than events that happened only days ago. She could almost feel the heat in the Sawchucks' kitchen with the sun shining through the window. On a warm day, the wood-burning cooking range kept the kitchen an inferno, and if the flies weren't too bad, the threshing crew ate outside on boards nailed together over sawhorses.

She recalled how aware she'd been then of all the men, their sidelong glances, their favourite desserts, their appetites. They were neighbours, working in a gang to harvest each of their farms in turn. She knew every one of them, including Orest from when he'd attended school, didn't mind their teasing as she poured coffee and slid biscuits onto their plates, breathing in the smell of sweat, grain chaff, machine and hair oil mingling with roast chicken or cabbage rolls. Max still had all her secret attention, with his wide shoulders and luxurious moustache, his bear-like presence, usually laughing when he was with company. But Eleanor once heard him sing "The Song of the Volga Boatmen" for his neighbours so beautifully, his voice full of such deep power and sorrow, she stood mesmerized with tears in her eyes and the potato knife frozen in her hand until Anna confiscated it and started peeling.

How sensible she'd been for her age. But no, part of all that had been plain fear: she wasn't sure enough of herself. At any rate, going home was the best thing she could have done. Wasn't it? she asked Olivia. It certainly was, Olivia would tell her. Seventeen was no age to start an affair with a married man. Or with anybody, for that matter.

She realized it was already time for dinner. She always tried to get to the dining room early on Sundays so she could hold a table for the other three. The other two. Well, actually four now, since Andrew and Palmer often joined them. She sped up to pass Tillie Johnson, a ninety-five-year-old using a walker. She was an old acquaintance from the days of volunteering for the CCF. "Hello, Tillie," she said. Tillie nodded grimly and she stopped. Next week, Tillie was scheduled to move up to the second floor. "So, are you all ready for the move?" She knew she sounded inane, but felt she ought to say something.

"As ready as I'll ever be," Tillie said. Her face was small and wrinkled as a dried apple. She continued grimly on her way. Several other people said hello now, commenting blandly on the weather as they passed Eleanor, eager to see what was on offer for the big meal of the week. She turned absently to thank someone who'd stopped to let her through first and was startled to see Donald Eston nodding politely. His bushy eyebrows sheltered grey eyes that seemed to hold nothing but ordinary courtesy.

With Olivia's death, Eston and his sins had been pushed aside. And now she didn't want to be preoccupied with anything other than her romance with Andrew. The excitement and comfort, the pleasure of anticipation. Death had interrupted but also heightened it, somehow, and she certainly wasn't about to let Donald Eston ruin everything.

Eston continued to frequent the lounge and dining room, looking benign and unconcerned, treating everyone with the same politeness. Eleanor had become almost used to his presence, ignoring him in the lineup for coffee, passing him in the hallway. She noticed him sitting in the lounge now and then with Bea Armitage, although Bea never managed to sit still for more than a few minutes. They seemed to talk mostly about the bird, and it was encouraging that he was never around when Chandra was visiting. Maybe that in itself was fishy, however, Eston conspicuously staying away from Chandra.

But she simply could not deal with those suspicions. Mrs. Brown knew that Bea was no more capable of babysitting an eight-year-old than Kilroy was. Dealing with Chandra should be Mrs. Brown's responsibility.

The next evening, when Thelma was feeling under the weather and couldn't play hearts, Eleanor found herself sitting at a card table with him.

She and Andrew were already there, waiting, when Palmer showed up, leading Eston toward the table like a host with a special guest.

"I had to do some arm twisting," Palmer said. "Donald here finally agreed to play after he figured out I'd be his only challenge."

"Ha!" Andrew grinned, handing Eston the deck as he sat down. "We'll see who challenges who."

"Whom," Eleanor said automatically. Her brain seemed to have shut down.

"Eleanor. You've been hanging around Fern too long," said Palmer.

Donald Eston shuffled and shuffled the cards. All the weeks she'd spent trying not to think of him, or attempting to think of him as innocent, came to nothing. She wondered, what if this were Clifford Olson or Paul Bernardo? Would she sit there playing cards? Whom would she refuse to play with? Mengele? "You know," she said, "I think I must be coming down with Thelma's flu, I don't feel at all well."

"I thought you looked pale," Andrew said. "And so quiet." Palmer agreed.

"I'll see you tomorrow." She stood, shakily reaching for her cane, which Eston handed to her, his eyes looking blandly from under eyebrows knit together with ordinary concern. A hideous scene from the book broke in on her, the father holding his hand over the girl's mouth while someone else…a rush of hatred almost knocked her back into her chair, and she grasped the edge of the table. Andrew was already standing, ready to provide a steady arm. "Don't bother," Eleanor said. "I'll be fine. Just a bit dizzy from getting up so fast." But he saw her out and insisted on walking her to her suite.

After he left, she went over to Fern's place. A cold autumn wind chilled her; the faux Victorian street lamps seemed to cast more shadow than light. Her ears were ringing with hate, her lungs, her very breath, full of it. Not all for Donald Eston though. A good part was for herself.

Fern answered her door, already in her housecoat. She was trying some new medication, she said, which helped suppress her palsy but made her sleepy. "What's wrong?" she asked, seeing Eleanor's expression.

"Something has to be done."

"About what?"

"I've just come from the lounge, where I almost played hearts with Donald Eston. Thelma's sick so Palmer got him as a replacement."

"Well." Fern didn't say anything, then shook her head. "This has got to stop. We have to stop thinking about this. I thought for a while Olivia's death might overshadow it for good."

"I don't even have the gumption to be rude to him," Eleanor said. "I said I didn't feel well." She sat down on Fern's grey loveseat. "I've forgotten about his crimes, or worse, accepted him as someone who's just there. I've become used to him."

Fern rubbed her forehead. "We should have done something about him a long time ago," she said. "At least tried to."

"I feel so debilitated I can't even think about it. It's as if I'm back in limbo after being sidetracked."

Fern was still standing, looking down at her. She went into the kitchen. "Do you want some tea?"

"No. Oh, maybe. Are you making some anyway?"

"Yes." Fern's voice had thickened with unshed tears. "I don't know why you feel your life is in limbo. You and Thelma have your men friends."

Eleanor ignored this. "As soon as Thelma's up and around we have to have a meeting."

Later that week Hallowe'en celebrations were held in the lounge. Various children dressed as cartoon or comic-book characters showed off their talents as Eleanor, Fern and Thelma sat at the back, grimly keeping an eye out. Eleanor was reminded of the three witches in *Macbeth*. Didn't they take their eyes out? Hand one eye around among the three of them? Or was that from a fairy tale? She looked over at Fern, but didn't have the heart to ask. Heart. Eyes.

Donald Eston walked into the room with Bea Armitage. A wave of exhaustion made Eleanor want to go home and sleep for a week. She could see Thelma and Fern watching him, alert, but she dozed until she heard the first notes of an accordion playing "Kalyna."

"Orest's dad used to dance to this, remember?" Fern asked. She turned to Thelma. "Max Sawchuck used to perform Ukrainian dance even in his seventies."

"Really?" Thelma looked over at Eleanor and smiled politely. Her lipstick today was new, Eleanor noticed, a matte crimson that stayed within the lines.

"Not really," Eleanor contradicted Fern. "He used to get drunk and dance at parties." He never "performed." Sometimes Fern had these silly ideas about people.

A sturdy, solemn little boy, maybe nine or ten years old, stood onstage in a Superman outfit playing his accordion with businesslike intensity. When he got to the lively chorus, he was a bit too slow for Eleanor's taste, but she was grateful to hear the polka they all used to dance to, not just at Ukrainian parties, but at weddings, no matter what the nationality, and at dances in the Legion Hall.

The silvery-green swirls on the boy's accordion caught the light as he looked briefly at the audience, ignoring his grandmother's little wave. Violet Gunderson was glowing with pride. She'd always looked more like a rose than a Violet, Eleanor thought. She felt a moment of kinship, nostalgic for her own grandson, even though he was well into his twenties. An image of his older sister teaching him how to use his tricycle came to her, sharp as a high-definition movie on TV. Jarret's fat little legs working the pedals, pushing the brand new cherry-red trike through the driveway gravel. Katya, patient as a little auntie, telling him how well he was doing.

A group of girls, dressed as various Disney princesses, giggled in the corner. Chandra was among them. Eleanor was glad to see someone had bought her a new outfit similar to the others', that she seemed to fit in so well. That she was well.

Thelma asked Corrine to come to their next meeting. Eleanor booked the boardroom. She thought a formal arrangement would be more effective, somehow; impress on Corrine the seriousness of the matter.

She was haunted by the Hallowe'en party, kept thinking of things that now struck her as suspicious. Who, for example, had bought Chandra the princess outfit? It angered her that she had to worry about some entertainment that a year ago would have been cause for nothing more than a desire for her grandchildren to start having children of their own before she wasn't there to see them. The memory of almost playing cards with Eston hit her with new intensity.

She carried a book to the meeting, but only for show. *Heart of Darkness*. When had they discussed it? Last April? They'd spent an entire meeting trying to interpret what Conrad was saying about evil. Eleanor had read it years before but hadn't remembered much. This time she'd found it disappointing, full of vague hints and ominous imagery with little substance for real discussion, until Fern pointed out that maybe Marlow wasn't a reliable narrator, and Olivia agreed. Thelma hadn't really understood their point. But maybe she was right, maybe Marlow was simply Conrad's mouthpiece.

As they followed Marcia, the activity coordinator, down the narrow corridor toward the centre of the Manor, they passed the exercise room. Eleanor felt a twinge in her knee. It had been weeks since she'd gone for therapy.

Marcia was obviously pleased they were starting up their book club meetings again. She unlocked the door to the boardroom and said, "I'll show your special guest in here as soon as she arrives."

"Thank you," Thelma said, "but she's already at my place freshening up. You don't have to trouble yourself, I think she knows the way."

"No trouble at all." Marcia's smile gleamed in the fluorescent light as she slipped away.

Eleanor wondered why Marcia, who was slender and dark, always seemed to give an impression of bulk. Maybe it was her clothes, always casual outfits with elastic waistbands and loose jackets. She clicked the door shut after her. "Corrine can knock," she said shortly.

Thelma looked up, then cleared her throat. "I can't believe you're still mad at Corrine," she said. "We've invited her here so we can get on with it. Maybe she can help us get on with actually doing something."

Eleanor sat down and poured herself some tea. The only air in the room was coming from the heating vent and seemed to lack oxygen. "Olivia's passing has put us in such an abject state…" She became too agitated to continue. "I felt I'd sunk so low when I found myself on the verge of playing cards with him… And of course there's Chandra…" She couldn't seem to finish her sentences.

"You know what?" Thelma said. "I figure he wouldn't dare touch any kid here. Not after getting that note of mine. He's been aware for a long time now that somebody knows about him. That he has to be careful."

"Careful isn't the same as not doing anything," Eleanor said. Thelma had always attached too much importance to that stupid note.

There was a light tap at the door. Corrine came in, looking distracted and slightly nervous. As she greeted them, she chose an oak chair next to her mother. "Hello, Corrine," Fern said politely. "Nice to see you again."

"Yes," Corrine smiled at her. "Same here."

Thelma poured her daughter some tea. "Eleanor wants to strangle you," she said. "To kill the messenger, I'd say."

With Corrine sitting right across from her, Eleanor's anger fizzled. "Yes, well, I'm upset with myself, really. A while ago, I was expected to play cards with that man, and all I did was give a polite excuse and leave. And of course there are children around. A child we've had to start worrying about." She found herself fired up again. "If you hadn't asked us to read that book, we'd be able to live our lives peacefully, as we want to at our age. My opinion is, the ball should be thrown back in your court entirely. We admit failure, but we also feel something ought to be done."

"I hadn't thought you'd feel such responsibility to actually do anything about him." Corrine looked down at the table, tracing the fake woodgrain with her finger. "I told you about him for your own safety, for your visitors' safety. Living next to someone like that…you should know." She looked abruptly at Eleanor. "Would you rather be ignorant of it all? Let that child you're so concerned about watch out for herself?"

This point being true only served to make Eleanor upset again. "And how much better off is she now? Have we been able to do anything? This knowledge has done nothing but ruin our lives."

"Oh, come on," Thelma said. "You've been doing quite well for yourself."

Fern was whispering, shaking her head and gesticulating, and fiddling with one of her earrings.

"Fern." Eleanor ignored Thelma altogether. "What do you think we ought to do?"

"What do I think?"

"Yes," Thelma put in. "Should we just give up and hope Corrine can try to get rid of him?"

Fern focussed her attention and said, "Yes. It's not only our own states of mind we're worrying about. As Eleanor said, there's a child. He seems to have made friends with a woman with dementia who has a great-granddaughter. The little girl visits regularly. It's a concern."

"To put it mildly," said Eleanor.

Fern, still fidgeting with her earring, said, "I think, Corrine, maybe you could get your women's group involved. Lobby the Pleasant Manor executive. At least get him out of here."

Corrine again looked down at the table. "I guess I could send a letter. Threaten to write to the papers naming Pleasant Manor as a harbour for superannuated perverts." She examined her fingernails, which, Eleanor noticed for the first time, were cut square. "We could all sign it," Corrine added.

"Leave me out," Eleanor said definitely. "I'm just worn down. We've discussed how the rest of the community here would feel about us if we were the ones to expose him. Not to mention that Eston himself would soon know who'd done it. Maybe we should have taken our chances and protested publicly right from the beginning and he might be out of here by now. But it's too late."

Thelma had become unusually silent, her eyes hooded. Corrine turned to her. "Mom? Will you at least sign the letter?"

Thelma shrugged. "Maybe I will. It won't make much difference to me; I'm not going to be here much longer."

"What?" Good God, Eleanor thought. Cancer?

"I'm moving out with Palmer," Thelma continued. "We're taking a bus tour to Las Vegas and Nashville in January, and then house-sitting his oldest daughter's condo in Calgary until next winter. Then we'll see."

They were all too astonished to say anything until Corrine croaked, "You're what?"

"I'm going on a trip with Palmer and then moving to Calgary with him."

Corrine glared at her bitterly. "God. If you knew the trouble I had getting you in here, and now... now you're just... taking off? With *Palmer*?"

"Thelma, Thelma." Fern was shaking her head, but smiling.

Eleanor didn't know how to respond. "Why didn't you say anything?" she asked. She felt disregarded, surprisingly bereft. Even though she hadn't become close to Thelma, she had become a chum of sorts, someone to go on double dates with.

"We only decided last week. That's why I told you I had the flu. I had to think things out by myself." She spooned sugar into her tea. "Olivia passing away like that really threw me for a loop. I decided I could be next and that it was time to live some more, seize the day and gather ye rosebuds and all that."

"You won't last," Eleanor said bluntly. "You find Palmer irritating now, I can tell. What's it going to be like in a year?"

"I like my men irritating," Thelma said. "It fits in with my world view. The openly annoying ones are trustworthy because they're not as likely to come up with mean surprises."

"That's ridiculous," Eleanor said, then realized how rude she was being, and shut up. Everyone was silent. "Oh," she said finally, "I'm just not feeling positive right now, about anything. Of course I wish you well, and not only that, I like Palmer and I'm sure you'll be happy enough." And in fact, this was true too. Not to mention that Palmer was someone who could afford to pay for a trip to Las Vegas and beyond. Not to mention, Eleanor realized, now Thelma could leave Pleasant Manor and Donald Eston far behind.

Corrine looked as if someone had knocked her on the head. "Mom," she said, getting up and nodding toward the door. "We have to talk."

Thelma looked at her. "I've said all I need to."

"There are issues we haven't touched on," Corrine said, "that you don't even recognize."

"Issues?" Thelma made a face.

"Corrine," Fern said. "Your mother is still healthy. She wants to live what she has left of life. As we all would like to."

Corrine continued to stand by the door waiting for her mother, who finally joined her. "All right," Thelma said. She nodded to Fern and Eleanor. "I'll see you both later for a drink, okay?"

"Fine," Eleanor said. "Corrine, I hope you're not going to forget about Donald Eston." Corrine waved at her, as if she were already quite a distance away. She and her mother left the room.

"Well. How about that? What a …." Eleanor's mind seemed able to toss out nothing but inane fragments.

"Only two of us left now," Fern said.

Eleanor's resentment began to rise again. "You know, this is only what I'd expect from Thelma. She's escaping, abandoning us to deal with Eston on our own, even though she and her daughter started it all. We should never have let her into our group in the first place."

Fern looked down. "Olivia and I knew you didn't like Thelma much, but we thought, well…" Her voice trailed away. "There was no harm in her, and she was so keen."

"Pushy, you mean."

"It would have been unpleasant to refuse and we thought it would work out for the best. It did, for a while, didn't it? You and Thelma eventually got along fine, especially in a foursome with your men friends. Besides, three people don't make up much of a club."

A faint sense of satisfaction dawned as Eleanor realized Thelma would actually be gone, but she said, "Well, it's better than two." For a moment, she thought perhaps they could keep the club alive. They could change the topic, discuss anything under the sun. "Maybe now we can invite Andrew. He reads. He keeps up with things."

Fern didn't look enthusiastic. "Maybe there are other women out there who might be interested in joining us."

"Oh Christ," Eleanor said. Fern laughed. They both got to their feet slowly, as if standing up had become a great effort.

"Maybe you should see what Andrew thinks, though," Fern said.

"About joining our group?"

"No. About Donald Eston. Get a male point of view. Maybe he'd have some ideas. In case Corrine and her letter don't pan out."

"Tell Andrew?" She recalled considering it at one time. "It's strange, but I've never said a thing to him about any of it. I guess I thought it might ruin things, bringing in something so ugly."

"We need another opinion."

"I talked to Dennis and Beth about it once, earlier on."

"You did?"

"Yes. They were no help at all, just told me it was best to mind my own business."

"Beth too?" Fern asked, surprised.

"She was thinking about the horrible botch-up the Saskatoon police made investigating that daycare in the early nineties. Lives were ruined. False accusations about something like this — it's a terrible thing."

"It can't hurt to ask Andrew. Just to see if he has any suggestions."

"Yes. I will."

Even as the days grew colder, Eleanor and Andrew often took short walks outside on the sidewalk surrounding the Manor. There'd been a brush of November snow, but the path was swept and perfect for a stroll, except for the fact that it was fifteen below. "We'll be outside less than half an hour," Andrew said, noting her long down-filled parka, the hood covering half her face, her thick knit scarf.

"I know. I can't take the cold at all anymore. Especially when winter's just starting."

He was wearing a light toque barely covering his ears and a duffel coat. "You need a scarf," she said, and went back inside to grab one from her bedroom closet before he could argue. She was struck by how small and unwelcoming her bed looked, how insufficient and barren the room seemed.

As they began their walk, she caught sight of Hannah Sundine huddled into a fur coat, making her way to the Manor for coffee but stopping for a long moment to stare at Eleanor and her man friend. No wonder Thelma and Palmer were going away. She should be thankful for plain companionship, she thought. She'd certainly spent enough time trying to convince herself she preferred it this way.

Romantic companionship. Maybe that's what she should call it. They had managed to find opportunities to kiss again, but felt so rushed they were unable to go any further. There was no way of visiting each other without the whole community observing them, so they kept their visits too short for speculation.

Because of the cold, they moved slightly faster than usual. "It just occurred to me," he said, "maybe you shouldn't be outside at all. What with rheumatism in your knee and that. And what about that night you had that dizzy spell?"

"Oh no, I'm fine now; and my knee's been better lately." She tightened her mittened grip on his arm. "In fact, since that evening I've been meaning to talk to you about something." She knew this sounded ominous. She had the mad thought that if they were fifty years younger this conversation would sound like a pregnancy scare. A short bark escaped her, and she cleared her throat.

"What is it?" He bent to look at her, attempting to see her expression inside her hood.

"There's a rumour going around about Donald Eston," she said, "which unfortunately I'm inclined to believe. Have you heard anything?"

"No." He looked mystified. "Nothing at all."

"Really, it's much more than a rumour." She told him everything. She summarized pertinent scenes from the book, trying to get the bald facts across without too much description. By this time, they'd almost made the complete circuit.

"My God. I don't know what to say." He was appalled. "It can't be true," he said finally.

"You should read the book and come to your own conclusions." They came to her door. Snow was falling. They hesitated, letting the crystals gather on their shoulders. "Come in for a cup of tea," she said.

He shook his head. "The biddies are watching out their windows." He looked withdrawn as he handed her the scarf. "I'll see you this evening. This is something I have to think about."

"All right." She closed the door. But instead of taking her coat and boots off, after a few minutes she went out again, back to the Manor. She found Fern in the lounge, sitting on a hard chair facing a clear window. Eleanor pulled a chair up beside her, and they watched the snow falling. When it reached a few centimetres in depth, Murray the caretaker, ponderous and intent, swept it away.

"I told him."

Fern didn't need to ask what or whom. "And?"

"He's concerned, of course. But really, I think it's something he'd rather not know about."

"I see."

They watched Murray sweep layer after layer onto the snowdrifts beside the walk so that people in walkers and wheelchairs could continue to come and go. Eleanor was reminded of a Greek myth. What was it? "Who was that Greek who was condemned to push the stone up the mountain forever?"

"Sisyphus."

"Yes."

When she saw Andrew the next day, the temperature was twenty below and falling so they stayed in, walking the Manor hallway. The evening before, he hadn't been able to talk to her alone, but now, speaking out of the side of his mouth as if he were in a spy movie, he said, "All I can come up with is to ask him outright. He'd deny it, and that would be that, except there'd be hard feelings. I'm not going to make trouble for no good reason."

Relieved he was mentioning Eston at all, she asked, "Do you want to read the book?" She knew the answer but felt obliged to ask.

"No." He stopped and looked at her. "Eleanor. He's never had any charges laid against him. He'd deny it and I'd believe him. He seems decent to me. He's an ordinary man."

Bea Armitage zoomed past them with Kilroy clutching her shoulder. "Honk honk," she said. "Coming through."

"It's okay." Eleanor patted his arm. "Maybe we've been making too much of it." She regretted letting him know about it. All his reaction proved was that he was unexceptional, as spineless as many men were about that kind of thing. But of course, what about herself? Wasn't she the one who was so upset with Corrine for giving them that book to read? Would she have read it, given the choice?

For that matter, Andrew could be right. This thought caught her up short for a moment. Maybe Eston's innocence really was possible. After all, Fern had thought so too. Andrew had been in the army during the war, and he'd dealt with men all his life in his hardware store. He knew a lot more about men than she did, so why should she dismiss his judgement out of hand? Wouldn't Andrew be able to recognize evil if it were there?

She began to watch Eston now for reassuring evidence of innocence, for those signs of normal humanity she'd noticed previously and questioned. The next time she saw him and Bea together, she asked herself to assume he was paying attention to Bea and her bird out of simple kindness. She passed close by them, ostensibly making her way to the couch to watch TV. The bird was pecking at Bea's fingernails, alternating a liquid cooing sound with his old lady cough. He ignored Eston altogether, as he did most men.

"That cough is the only thing Kilroy ever learned," Bea was telling him. "Chester could say 'Pieces of eight.' I don't know who taught him that."

"Chester?" Eston's voice seemed kind, normal. Or was it a bit too sympathetic, a bit overdone?

"Little Chester. Kilroy's buddy. He was so chirpy and perky, no one knew he was sick until he just up and died." Bea didn't seem too upset at the memory.

"Just up and died, eh?" Eston sounded vaguely sardonic, a bit irritated, as most men would be dealing with someone like Bea.

But then why deal with her at all? Eleanor sat down. Staring blindly at Oprah weeping with someone over a lost relative, she tried again to eavesdrop on Bea and Eston. He was murmuring now, on purpose, it seemed to her, but of course her hearing wasn't what it used to be. She did not feel reassured.

10

Trapped but comfortable in a low armchair of imitation suede, Eleanor held up her glass for more New Year's champagne. She usually didn't remain with Dennis and Beth past Boxing Day, but this year they had invited her to extend her visit. They'd decided to have a quiet celebration at home, and Eleanor was content to stay, although she thought she might have had a better time at the Legion party with Andrew. She was disappointed her grandchildren hadn't made it home for any part of the holidays. Katya and Jarret each had live-in sweethearts from opposite ends of the country. "Partners," they called them. Both had agreed to spend Christmas with their partners' families.

"Here's to all my resolutions." Dennis was jovial and red in the face; he'd been nipping rye and water the whole evening. Champagne was dessert.

"But you're so perfect, dear. Why would you even bother to make resolutions?" Beth eyed the front of his good shirt stretched taut by his expanding beer gut. She was looking elegant in a black blouse and pants, her shoulders wrapped in an oriental shawl embroidered with peacocks.

Eleanor didn't blame her for being a bit sarcastic. Whenever she hadn't seen Dennis for a while, she was hit with mild jolt of surprise at finding him so heavy. So middle-aged. As a teenager, Dennis had been dangerously handsome. Tall and broad-shouldered with fine but pronounced features, he could have become a heartbreaker if he'd wanted to, but he'd been entirely unaware. He slouched and mooched and teased, he dressed like a slob and liked to wrestle with friends, play team sports and inflict practical jokes. Girls would phone him up and he'd mumble a few monosyllables at them, rather rudely, she would admonish him, but he'd shrug his shoulders and go back to his book or TV show.

By the time he let Beth land him he'd been safely on his own for several years, and Eleanor had long quit worrying. After his marriage he gained weight and grew into his personality: a big, easygoing farmer who liked to curl and watch hockey games and joke around. Of course he was more complicated than that: he read history books; he worried about his kids; he drank too much; he thought the demise of the family farm was a tragic mistake the world would soon regret.

She raised her glass in another toast to the New Year, feeling a rare kinship with Beth. "Remember the New Millenium?" she asked. "When Dennis stockpiled all that firewood and canned food?"

Beth laughed. "We're still eating beans from the year 2000. I think he was disappointed when Armageddon didn't happen."

Dennis grimaced at both of them and got up from the couch. "Armageddon some more snacks. You want anything?"

After he returned with potato chips and dip, Beth gave Dennis a serious look, and his expression sobered, rather grudgingly, Eleanor thought. She wondered what was up.

"So, Eleanor..." Beth hesitated. "We've been meaning to ask long before now. Have you found out anything more about that Ronald Eston?"

"Donald."

"What?"

"It's Donald Eston. No. Since Olivia died, we haven't had the strength. It's like you said. It's none of our business, and we can't do anything anyway."

"Did we say that?" She played with the fringe of her shawl. "I guess, in a way it's true. It's just that I've been thinking about it, and wondered if there was something..." Her voice trailed away.

Too little too late, Eleanor thought. "There's a child who shows up at Pleasant Manor fairly regularly and we think he's shown some interest in her."

Beth looked dismayed. "No. Really?"

"Thelma's daughter said she was going to write a letter to Pleasant Manor. To complain, or at least make them aware of who he is, and then maybe they'll decide to ask him to leave. Or something. It will be up to them." What had happened to their opinion that Eston was likely falsely accused, Eleanor wondered?

"A friend of mine has read the book," Beth said. "She thought it was pretty convincing. Anyway, I'd be worried about kids visiting. It's... well, if I were in your shoes, I don't know what I'd do."

"If there's a kid involved, we should all be worried," Dennis said. "But it's New Year's Eve, for God's sake. Let's talk about it tomorrow."

Late the next day Eleanor sat as still as she could in the same armchair, nursing a headache and reviewing various other New Year's Days of her life. At least this year, comfortably settled in with only Dennis and Beth, she didn't have to worry about having done anything stupid the night before. A recollection rose murkily to the surface of the New Year's Eve she'd given Max a real kiss. All the neighbours had been over and everyone, having had far too much to drink, was kissing everyone else at midnight. Who was Orest kissing? She'd had just enough time to concentrate on Max. Oh lord. She sank down a little in her chair. She'd been so drunk she was able, the morning after, to convince herself she'd imagined it.

She looked over at Dennis, who was watching a review of the year's news on TV with a damp cloth on his forehead. He was built like his Ukrainian grandfather, but had developed the stomach that Max always seemed on the verge of acquiring but never had. Like Max, Dennis seemed to lack Orest's knowledge, his self-awareness.

She'd been married to Orest forty-seven years and it was a happy marriage. She didn't like to consider what she'd found attractive in Max. He'd been an impossible man. He would have been impossible to live with. She had no illusions about how Ukrainian men of Max's generation treated their women, knew she was lucky Orest had learned to identify with the generic benignity of Canadians.

She took a couple more Aspirin from the bottle Dennis had left on the coffee table. All that was so far in the past. She would look forward to the new year, try to be optimistic. She still had a life and she should make the best of it, still had some time to make new things happen. She was attempting to concentrate on the television when the phone rang.

"Mom, it's Fern." Dennis handed her a new cordless telephone, which she examined as if it were the control panel of a Concord jet. "Mom. I already pressed the button when I answered. Just talk. Say hello."

She gave Dennis a look. "Hello, Fern. Happy New Year!" She tried to sound hale and hearty.

"Eleanor, I have some bad news." Before Eleanor had time to digest this, Fern forged on. "Andrew has had an accident. He's... I think he'll be all right, but he fell on some ice."

Eleanor couldn't quite comprehend this. "What?"

"He's back here at the Manor in a wheelchair." Fern lowered her voice, as if she were calling from a public phone. "He may have to move to the second floor."

"Oh, God." Her headache was so bad now she knew she'd be no good to him today. "Tell him I'll be there tomorrow morning." Her hearing seemed to have deteriorated. She listened to Fern tell her a few more details through a barrier of cotton batting before she said goodbye and handed the phone back to Dennis.

"What's the matter?" he asked.

"My friend Andrew has fallen and hurt himself."

"Oh!" Dennis looked more upset than she would have thought necessary until she realized it was because she herself must look like death warmed over. A look passed between him and Beth.

"Aw, Eleanor," Beth said. "Isn't it just one thing after another?"

11

Andrew was sitting in a wheelchair behind the glass doors of the entrance, waiting for her. "Goddamn it, Eleanor, look at what I've been reduced to." She hung up her coat. Although distressed by his accident, she was somewhat gratified at his obvious reliance on her. This in turn was tinged with dismay. She'd expected him to be diminished somehow. Ill and morose. Instead he seemed larger: swollen and vigorous with anger.

"Andrew." She touched his hand, not knowing how much sympathy to show. "Let's get some coffee in the lounge; you can tell me what happened." She took hold of the wheelchair handles.

"Get your hands off that!" he snapped, turning the chair to face her.

She raised her eyebrows. All his courtly politeness had gone out the window. But instead of being upset, she felt more comfortable with him. Some sort of border was being crossed. Still, she didn't have to put up with this kind of behaviour. "Fine," she said, "I'll talk to you later, maybe." She gripped her cane and started off down the hall.

"Eleanor!" he called. She stopped. "Come back. Please." She stumped rather stolidly back to his side. "I'm behaving like a five-year-old," he said. He didn't sound very humble, but she relented.

"Yes, you are," she said. Feeling a rush of tenderness, she bent over him, her hand on his shoulder. He grabbed her hand with both of his, and they stayed like that for a long moment, until Palmer beckoned to them from the lounge.

Andrew wheeled himself over, Eleanor walking beside him. They settled at a table with Palmer and Thelma.

After chatting with Eleanor about her family, Palmer turned to Andrew, somewhat reluctantly. "So how are you doing?"

"As you can see," Andrew said.

"Oh, you'll be up and around again in no time," Thelma said, pouring the coffee. Eleanor stopped herself from clicking her tongue with impatience.

"No, I won't." Now that it came to discussing his situation, Andrew's anger dissipated and his voice was deadpan, matter-of-fact. "This is it"— he indicated his wheelchair— "for the rest of my days."

"Huh." Palmer grunted as if someone had punched him. "I thought you said there wasn't anything broken."

"No, it's just the same old problems made worse. My leg is worse; I can hardly move it, and my back's hurt now too. I'm too old for rehab."

They all concentrated on stirring their coffee. Finally Eleanor nodded somewhat awkwardly toward Thelma and Palmer and said, "So how about these two?"

"How about what?" Andrew asked suspiciously, looking at Palmer.

"Their leaving Kasokinaw. Their trip to the southern States. "

"Oh, that," Andrew said. "Yes, I say good for you, taking off out of here to fine weather." He glanced at Eleanor. "You can take us along with."

Thelma and Palmer chatted about their plans over second cups of coffee. Thelma showed them the brochures for the tour.

Creasing one of them to make a paper airplane, Palmer cleared his throat. "We were thinking, uh, my niece here in town will be gone too. See, her and Leanne are going to Europe together. They both have work over there. Or Leanne does and Nancy is taking time off to study or something. We could have house-sat for either one of them. They're both single again. So, well now, you know Nancy's house here will be empty."

After an awkward silence, Thelma said, "So if you two, or, uh, either one of you…" She trailed off for a moment. "If you want to go over there now and then, we'll leave you a key."

"To look after it?" Eleanor was a bit apprehensive.

"No, no, a neighbour does that. Just for if you want to get away on your own. From the gossip hens." Palmer's beefy face took on the hue of overripe cherries, and he looked off into a space somewhere between Andrew and Eleanor. He gave Andrew's wheelchair a sideways glance. "As soon as you feel up to, uh, going anywhere again."

Furious at herself for blushing too, Eleanor looked down at her coffee. She couldn't think of a thing to say.

"Right," Andrew said. "Well. Thank you kindly."

"We'll miss hearing you read for Robbie Burns Day." Thelma, unusually tactful, changed the subject.

"Och, Robbie Burns," Andrew said, exaggerating his accent, "I'll be reading him nae more."

"Why not?" Eleanor asked. "You didn't injure your vocal chords. And," she toned down her impatience, "you recite so well, Andrew."

"What's that one you did last year?" Thelma asked.

"*A man's a man, for a' that and a' that,*" Palmer contributed in an inept brogue.

Andrew shook his head. "If you'll excuse me," he said, "I'll be back in a minute." They watched as he wheeled himself fairly proficiently out of the lounge toward the washroom.

Thelma nodded to Palmer. "Maybe you can go with him, see if he needs any help. Stand outside the washroom, just make sure he knows you're there. You know he won't ring for anyone unless he's half dead." The bathrooms were all equipped with emergency buzzers.

Palmer looked hesitant, then trailed reluctantly after Andrew.

"Tsk." Thelma shook her head, watching him. "On second thought, I guess he'd call for a nurse's aide a hell of a lot sooner than he'd ever call on Palmer."

"Thelma," Eleanor said. "We're not going to be using Nancy's house."

"Oh, but it would be wheelchair accessible," Thelma said, "or at least since Andrew can stand a bit on his good leg, he can get in and out of the van and Murray can help him. It's a walk-in bungalow. And the bathroom is nice and big enough." She brightened slyly. "Wait till you see the tub. It's a Jacuzzi."

"You mean we should book the van from Pleasant Manor? Get *Murray* to drive us to someone's empty house? Not very likely."

"Aw, Eleanor. Say you're visiting someone. Or take the taxi. Those wheelchairs fold up, you know. You can just throw it in the trunk. For that matter, once the snow clears I bet you're strong enough to wheel Andrew over there yourself and check it out. It's only a few blocks. If you're just not up to this, fine, but you can find a way if you want." She blew a little wavelet onto her coffee, took a brief sip.

"You two are physically spry, if nothing else," Eleanor said. "You have no idea what it means, not being able to get around easily. And look at Andrew now, for Pete's sake."

"Oh, I know." Thelma made a move as if to pat Eleanor's arm, but didn't. "I expect nothing will happen and that's the sensible way to be. But he can still stand up when he wants to; I saw him get out of a car yesterday. That comment about being too old for rehab is bunk."

Eleanor didn't reply. Waiting for the men to return, she gazed through the window and watched a black dog lope lazily down the sidewalk.

Thelma and Palmer had their meagre households packed up and moved into storage by the following week, and drove off to Calgary in Palmer's Cutlass Supreme. As with Olivia, in the end they left no trace of their existence. Within another week or two, their suites were taken over by new residents, and they'd taken off on their American gambling and country music expedition.

The weather was warm for February, almost above freezing, and Eleanor and Andrew went out for fresh air several afternoons in a row. Having Andrew's wheelchair to lean on, Eleanor didn't need her cane.

That afternoon, she wore a wool scarf tied loosely over her ears, and Andrew looked jaunty in an Andy Capp hat. They circled the Manor, chatting casually, comfortable. They'd become good friends, Eleanor realized. She looked at the clear salt-strewn path in front of them, remembering with regret the times they'd walked together before Andrew's fall, holding on to each other side by side. "It's too bad the Legion doesn't take better care of its parking lot."

Andrew was silent for a moment. "I didn't really slip on any ice," he said.

"What do you mean? You certainly hurt yourself somehow."

"Yes. I just… Well, the fact is, I just fell over."

"What?"

"Yes. Out of the blue. I fell over, for no reason I can see. I said it was ice, but that's not true. I noticed a patch and avoided it."

"Whatever happened, here you are, ice or no ice. It could have been worse. You're lucky you didn't break your hip."

He looked up at her, annoyed. "In case you hadn't noticed, my girl, I'm right crippled."

"Oh for heaven's sake. I meant you're not, I mean you don't seem to be in much pain, that's all."

"As long as I don't try to walk."

"Well, maybe you should be trying. Are you sure exercise won't help at all?"

"Och. Ye're as bad as the doctor. I'm not goin' for therapy. I'm too old. Why put myself through all that crap?"

Eleanor stopped walking. "Do you mean to tell me you're *supposed* to be trying to walk? Getting therapy?"

He was silent, looking angrily across the street, watching a ginger cat step its way furtively into a garage.

"Well?" Then she caught herself and started to push the chair again.

"Never mind," she said. "It's your own business and I'd likely do the same." Though she couldn't help but think that she hadn't. After her own fall, she'd begun therapy almost immediately. And didn't he realize that with no improvement he might end up on the second floor? He'd managed on his own so far, though Mrs. Brown did send an aide over to check up on him and help him with baths.

"Eleanor," he said as they started up the walk to the front of the Manor. "I have the key in my pocket."

"What key?"

"To Palmer's niece's place. Nancy. She's gone now."

Eleanor couldn't think of a thing to say.

"Look," he pointed down the empty street as if he wanted to make a getaway. "Run in and grab your cane if you want it," he said urgently. "I'll phone the cab."

Run in, she thought, irritated. "Andrew," she said. But they made their way inside and she parked him near the phone at the empty front desk.

"Maybe we'll go out to The Gem for supper afterwards," he called. She collected her cane from the umbrella stand. After what? She didn't take time to think. Seeing Mrs. Brown stalk purposefully toward her, she said awkwardly, "I'm, uh, Andrew Stuart and I are going out for a while."

But busy and preoccupied, Mrs. Brown continued down the hall. "Fine, dear, fine," she called. Before Andrew's accident Eleanor wouldn't have had to consider telling Mrs. B. anything. Her mouth turned dry as she saw the town's only taxi already turning into the driveway.

Fred Kanske, the driver, folded and stashed the wheelchair in the trunk while Andrew, surprisingly able, stood and moved on his own to the front seat. "Come on, come on!" he beckoned to her as if they'd just robbed a bank. "We don't have all day."

Oh, hell. She got in the car and strapped herself in.

"All aboard?" Fred winked at her in his rear-view mirror, radiating the false joviality people assume when they have to deal with the handicapped and elderly. Eleanor was too excited to resent this.

"Nancy Durocher's house on Birch Avenue," Andrew said, too slyly.

Bea Armitage's face appeared, floating beside the car window as if it were connected to a string. Eleanor opened the window slightly in an attempt to be kind. "Hi Bea," she said.

"Sneaking off for a bit of nookie, eh?" Bea said, squinting in at her with a clear, distinctly malevolent, look.

"What?" But before Eleanor could come back with a comment about Bea's state of mind, she realized it had already returned to its fog. Her eyes had regained their vacancy, her expression was once again innocuous. Eleanor closed the window. "Who on earth let her outside?" she asked.

Andrew was having a fit of laughter, and the cab driver, pretending he hadn't heard anything, concentrated on phoning their destination in to his wife, whom he referred to as central headquarters. He drove the few blocks to the house, briskly helped Andrew back in his chair and through the doorway of the bungalow. Still embarrassed, Eleanor thought he drove off looking far too cheerful.

Inside, she leaned on her cane, feeling as if she'd just run a marathon. She tried to control her breathing and gazed self-consciously at the living room: the velveteen chesterfield, the orange geometric pattern on the curtains, the pseudo-Berber carpet. "I'm only curious, you know, as to what the place looks like," she said, and then felt stupid.

Laughter seemed to have wiped anything tentative from Andrew's manner. Bea's comment had given him a certain confidence, a new perspective on the entire enterprise. "Yes." He nodded, putting the key back in his jacket pocket. He took in everything, including Eleanor, with a proprietary glance.

A mixed wave of terror, anticipation, and sudden and extreme annoyance left her frail and unsteady. She glared at Andrew, thinking this whole situation was ridiculous. He reached over and grasped her hand. "Eleanor," he said. His voice was reassuring and slightly reproving. He turned her hand in his two, and kissed the inside of her wrist. She didn't look at him. She took their coats to hang in the closet, then sat down in the living-room chair closest to the entrance.

Andrew wheeled himself over to the couch and set the brakes. He lifted himself, wincing in pain but determined, stood for a moment and actually took a couple of steps before he settled in. He beckoned to Eleanor. "Come and sit with me." She did, patting her hair in place, wondering what she looked like. Feeling warm, she took off her cardigan. "We'll take it so slowly, maybe nothing will happen at all," he said, putting his arm around her shoulders and pointing his chin toward the bedroom. With his back the way it was, maybe nothing *could* happen. Eleanor found this thought reassuring, if something of a letdown. She leaned against him, contemplating the picture window: the white lawn surrounded by a brown stick hedge, the frost patterns melting on the little windows at the side. She was acutely aware that Andrew had taken control and that this was just what she wanted.

His hand closed around the bare flesh of her upper arm. "Ahh," he breathed out harshly, as if touching her there was enough. "Skin like silk." Lust, hovering somewhere in her periphery, began to hone in. Orest used to say that about her skin. Who knows, she thought, maybe it would always be true.

Andrew managed to make his way into the bedroom without the wheelchair, using Eleanor's cane and a determination they didn't think to laugh about until later. They made love. Having to move carefully became, in the end, excruciatingly exciting.

Afterwards, her flesh felt expanded, plumped with pleasure. They ate canned chicken soup for a late supper and called the cab, attempting to tone down their expressions. "You look like the cat that's swallowed the canary," Eleanor said.

"Ah, no, my girl." He put on his thickest accent. "I'm the Cheshire cat, who will seduce ye further and further into wickedness." Eleanor laughed. She wanted to stay the night, but then remembered her partial plate and didn't suggest it.

The only person they met outside Pleasant Manor that evening was Donald Eston. He'd been to the library, and carried a bag of books. He greeted them briefly, so hunched over he had to contort his neck to say hello. She couldn't bring herself to feel anything about him right then, and the idea of his innocence, no longer a mental exercise but an actual impression, darted across her mind like a small, unexpected animal.

Fern visited Eleanor, or had coffee with her and Andrew in the lounge, but otherwise kept to herself. She rarely walked for exercise anymore. The medication suppressed her palsy but continued to drain her of life. "I think you should see the doctor again," Eleanor told her. She'd just come upon Fern whispering, sitting on a chair near the main entrance. Her hair floated like gossamer against the light from the glass doors, her earrings cast tiny mercurial prisms.

"Doctors. I've had enough of them," Fern said. She seemed to be continuing her own conversation. "I want to fade away now, in peace."

Eleanor looked down at the green tile. "Oh, Fern."

"You know," Fern said, "if I could work myself up to it, I'd go and talk to him."

"To whom?"

"Donald Eston."

Eleanor took a sharp breath. She was sick. Sick to death of being reminded of him. "Why on earth would you want to do that?"

"I just … I've started thinking about him again, all the time. I try to watch when kids are around. I saw Chandra again the other day. Did you know she still comes here alone?"

"Yes." Eleanor had deliberately pushed Chandra out of her mind.

"I walk behind him in the hallway or see his face at another table and I think 'is it true or not?' I keep thinking I'd be able to tell if I asked him outright."

"Oh, God. I don't think so. He'd naturally be angry and horrible; who knows, he might even, oh, I don't know. Try to hit you or something. After Thelma's note and all." She remembered Andrew saying that was the only thing he'd be able to do, to ask him outright, to talk to him. But of course he hadn't.

"But if he *is* guilty, he should be held to account," Fern said. "He should have been punished by law a long time ago, not just by gossip from readers of his daughter's book. And not only Eston. Someone should be nosing around that town, trying to find out who those other men were. Her book describes a judge, a priest, that politician who always used to be on TV, and God knows how many others. It's … I can't even think of a strong enough word. It's *hideous* that those people should be living out their lives with no consequences. In fact, *there's* some detective work for Corrine and her group."

"Some powerful people could be implicated," Eleanor said, "according to the book. If any of it is true, nosing around like that could be dangerous."

"That's going a bit far," Fern said.

"You don't think a judge or politician who's capable of paying to rape a child wouldn't be corrupt enough to threaten someone's life? Or know whom to hire?"

Fern was silent, then said. "I think we've been forgetting when all this happened. Those men are likely dead now. Or close to it." She stared out the window. "On the other hand, maybe none of it is true. Maybe none of it happened. What do you think of Eston now that he's been around here this long? Do you think it possible he might be innocent?"

"That's the thing." She recalled her impression the other night. She'd been hoping to tell Fern about her afternoon with Andrew, but now here was Eston again, floating to the surface like something ghastly and bloated. "I'm not sure any more. But I think my doubt might be a sort of evasion. I feel guilty for not watching him anymore, but I want just to survive and spend time with Andrew, to put the whole thing away. And whatever I think, I'm still waiting for Corrine to do something. I thought she was supposed to be taking over. I've abdicated any responsibility and so should you. We're too old."

Following Fern's gaze out the window, she saw a flock of waxwings descend onto a small highbush cranberry poking out of a snowdrift by the sidewalk. Its red fruit hung from the sparse branches like holiday decorations. Glad of the distraction, she watched as the chubby grey and tan birds gobbled the berries, their crests bobbing dementedly. With their black masks and air of recklessness, they looked like cartoon bandits. "Isn't it a bit late for cedar waxwings?" she asked.

"They're Bohemian waxwings," Fern informed her. "They just show up wherever and whenever there's food." After several minutes of gorging themselves, a few of the birds hopped awkwardly from the branches onto the cleared cement, where they sat immobilized like fat monks after a banquet, or bumbled into each other for short squabbles.

"There's something wrong with them."

"Oh dear," said Fern. "The berries were fermented. We'd better find Mrs. Brown's hawk."

Mrs. Brown had a black cut-out of a hawk she put up now and then on the glass doors to deter birds from smashing into them. As they walked away, Eleanor heard two thumps in succession but didn't turn to look.

12

Spring finally came again, wetter than usual, and by June everyone was talking about climate change. Marcia, the activity coordinator, decreed the next few days to be Caribbean Week; maybe, Eleanor thought, in a superstitious effort to bring on summer weather. A series of Sidney Poitier movies were shown. Harry Belafonte albums were played over the sound system and one of the local teachers presented a slideshow of her holiday in Jamaica. A steel drum band was booked for entertainment that afternoon, and tables moved to the side to clear the floor for dancing.

"A steel drum band!" Eleanor said. "Maybe there'll be some Harry Belafonte lookalikes."

"Huh." Andrew touched her hand in mock jealousy.

"Don't count on it," Fern laughed, pointing at the poster. "It's a bunch of Shriners from Saskatoon."

Several jocular middle-aged white men trooped into the lounge to set up their equipment. Instead of the ungainly oil barrels Eleanor had expected, thick-sided bowls of stainless steel glinted, swinging on thin black supports. One of the musicians, glancing at the audience, smiled in surprise. "Miss Albany." He came over to their table and held out his hand to Fern, who shook it automatically. "Remember me?"

She regarded him blankly, then smiled. "You must be an old student, but I'm not as young as I once was."

"Of course, it's been forty years." He laughed. "I might have changed a bit, but I'd recognize you anywhere." He introduced himself. "Tony Anderchuck."

"Well!" Fern was trying to recall who he was while giving the impression she remembered. "And what do you do in Saskatoon?"

"Oh, I'm in sales," he said, rather enigmatically. "But this," he waved his arm at the band, "is what I'd like to do all the time."

"You used to bring your dog to school!" Fern blurted this out, happy to have finally placed him.

His expression softened with memory. "Yeah, he used to follow me and wait. Couldn't make him stay home. Old Jigsy."

After he settled in with the band, ready to play, Fern nudged Eleanor. "Tony." She nodded her head towards him. "Caught him blowing frogs up with a straw once and gave him the strap. I bet he remembers that." Eleanor caught a glimpse of Fern as she was forty years ago, someone who, as one of her former students told Eleanor, never put up with any shit.

The band started up in full force with "Day-O" and continued with standard Caribbean favourites almost non-stop until they launched into "Jamaican Farewell." People clapped and swayed with the music. A young orderly from the second floor shuffled a two-step over to Bea Armitage, enticing her to dance.

What the Shriners lost in attempting Caribbean accents, they gained in enthusiasm: their perspiring faces above the shiny steel instruments looked euphoric. There were several couples dancing now. Eleanor swayed slightly to the rhythm. She glanced over at Andrew tapping his fingers on the table and thought about how she used to dance with Orest. She remembered the time they tried to learn to jive at their nephew's wedding, completely embarrassing Dennis. She would give her right arm to be able to dance just one more time.

Bea and the orderly were really cutting the rug, keeping graceful time to the music, and her face glowed. She didn't look young, but she looked beautiful. Half the room was up and moving now; Eleanor was envious even of Violet Gunderson dancing with a woman friend, although they weren't very good. As they bounced by, she saw a shadow near the doorway move into the light. Donald Eston stood blocking the entrance but seemed to have no intention of coming in until he caught sight of Bea. He straightened his spine, smiled amiably and almost sauntered over to her. He tapped the orderly on the back, cutting in. The orderly, a rather pudgy young man, grinned, play-acting an old-fashioned bow, and Bea danced off with Eston, still sporting her beatific glow. Making an effort to stand straight, he danced very well.

"The place is hopping," Andrew said. Seeing that he was enjoying himself, Eleanor tried to relax again into something other than resignation. Andrew smiled and for a surreptitious moment, took her hand. Fern glanced at them, then glanced quickly away.

Eleanor had the passing thought that it was just as well Andrew couldn't dance either. She would hate to see him dancing with someone else, or to feel she was slowing him down. Fern wore the tense look she always had at dances, half hoping and half fearing someone would ask her. She only danced well when she'd had too much to drink.

Eston seemed tired already. Eleanor could see he found it an effort to stand upright, and that he was ready to quit when Hannah Sundine's husband cut in. What was his name? Karl. Hannah wasn't there, Eleanor noted. Bea was well on her way to being the belle of the ball.

Today it was more obvious than usual how attractive Bea was; maybe Eston was simply an ordinary man interested in women his own age. But would someone with all his marbles want to court someone with dementia? Maybe abusive men weren't interested in sex but in power. Maybe it was Bea he was interested in hurting.

As soon as Eston quit dancing, he left the room, still carrying himself straighter than usual, and it was then that Eleanor noticed Chandra standing in the doorway watching them all, half hidden in her secretive way. As Eston passed her, he put what seemed to Eleanor a proprietary hand on her head, just for a moment, and continued on his way.

The music seemed too loud now. *My heart is down, my head is turning around.* The room had acquired a surreal look, the aged dancers performing a ritual she no longer wished to be part of. She was glad when she saw Marcia catch the eye of the band leader and tap her wristwatch.

Once the band had departed, everyone hung about, exhausted, looking like marionettes who'd lost their puppeteer. Only Bea Armitage had any energy left. She let Kilroy out of his cage. After such an hour of music and excitement, he flew, ecstatically erratic, around the room for longer than usual, landing on windowsills, touching down briefly on people's heads before finally settling on her hand. She took off with him to patrol the hallway as vigorously as ever. "That bird is a menace," Fern said.

"Who?" Andrew asked, trying to be jocular. "Kilroy or Bea?"

By the time they made their way to the front entrance, Chandra had disappeared. But seeing Eston lay his hand on her head had produced in Eleanor a hard core of resolution. She'd thought of something she could do. She didn't know why none of them had thought of this before. She could talk to Chandra.

The girl looked up from watching a cartoon as Eleanor stood stiffly in front of her. "Hello, Chandra, how are you?" She felt as if she hadn't spoken to a child in decades.

"I'm fine," Chandra said. Rather guardedly, Eleanor thought, but it was likely because her effort at casual chat was so awkward.

She sat down beside her on the couch. "What are you watching?"

"*Sponge Bob*." Chandra eyed her with adult patience. "It's my favourite," she offered, deciding, Eleanor could see, to be generous. Her face had become rounded over the months, plainer than when Eleanor had first met her, and sensible looking.

During the commercial, Eleanor picked up the remote and pressed mute. "I want to ask you something about a friend of your Grandma Bea's," she said.

"A friend?" Chandra asked. She seemed to think this was amusing.

"That man who visits with her sometimes. Donald." Eleanor's throat closed over the name so that she had to repeat it. "Donald Eston."

"Oh. Him." Chandra looked noncommittal.

Eleanor made sure her voice was clear. "Have you ever been alone with Mr. Eston?" she asked.

"Donald?" Chandra seemed uncertain.

"Yes."

"I guess." She searched Eleanor's face for the right answer. "Not too often." Her expression closed, became watchful.

Eleanor felt completely at a loss. What could she ask? Has he ever molested you? "Do you like him? Like having him around?"

"I guess," she said. She picked up the remote and clicked on the sound.

Disappointed with herself, Eleanor decided she would have to take another approach. She would take Chandra upstairs to see Bea. She would warn Bea against him. Maybe something of this magnitude would get through to her, and maybe then Chandra too would get the message, listening in on adults talking. She waited until *Sponge Bob* was over and then, becoming abruptly decisive, she took Chandra's hand. "Let's go find your grandma." The girl didn't argue.

As they rode up to the second floor, she thought maybe she should be trying to contact the girl's mother. She knew it would be lucky if Bea remembered a thing she said. On the other hand, Bea seemed to recall everything to do with her bird. Maybe she still had a few brain cells working, enough to be left with some kind of awareness that Donald Eston meant trouble.

The second-floor hallway was full of people, pushing walkers at a snail's pace, drooping in wheelchairs, staring out the windows, or babbling to themselves. Despite the hospital standard of cleanliness, a faint smell of human waste and something unidentifiably noxious cut through the disinfectant. Eleanor tried not to look anyone in the eye, just followed Chandra, who was marching ahead. They passed the orderly who'd danced with Bea and Eleanor nodded to him. What was his name? He was pushing a wheelchair containing a skeletal man who seemed hardly more than a bundle of clothes. "Looking for Bea, are you?" The orderly smiled, his face so smooth and pink you'd think he didn't have a care in the world. "Keep heading down the hall," he said. "She's in room 209, getting ready to go downstairs."

"Good," said Eleanor. "We'll go with her."

"I know where her room is," Chandra called back scornfully.

They found Bea sitting on a bed near the door, putting on her running shoes. At least she can tie her own shoes, Eleanor thought. The sparse white room was fairly large, and Bea shared it with two other people. A hugely obese woman in what seemed to be a catatonic state overflowed a chair by the middle bed. The third inmate was sitting up in her bed near the window. She stared at Eleanor as she walked in. It was Tillie, their old ally with the CCF. Reaping the benefits of their fight for Medicare. "How are you, Tillie?" Eleanor could see how she was, and it wasn't good.

"Ready to die," Tillie said. "Ready and willing," she clarified. Chandra was examining her with that vague analytical look on her face, but Tillie ignored the girl altogether.

"Well. Good luck." Eleanor knew this wasn't even remotely appropriate but now couldn't think of anything to add to it. The sun shone just as brightly through these windows as it did through those downstairs. From up here, she had a better view of the grounds. Crows were pecking at something unidentifiable on the lawn. What was it that a flock of crows was called? She turned away. "Bea. I have to talk to you about something important."

"I'm coming, just a minute," Bea said cheerfully. "Hello, Chandra," she said, "are you still here?" Good, thought Eleanor, she was clearer than usual. Of course, no one could tell how long any of her better states of mind would last. Bea stood up and took off down the hallway. Chandra ran after her.

"You'll have to slow down," Eleanor called.

"We'll meet you in the lounge." Bea stopped for a second and tossed this off casually, as if people with important things to talk about wanted her attention every day.

Eleanor took one last helpless look at Tillie. "Goodbye," she said. The fat woman in the centre sat like a monolith absorbing the energy from the room. Tillie didn't respond either.

The elevator seemed much slower on its way down. Bea and Chandra had taken the stairs, but at least when Eleanor finally got to the lounge they were there, waiting. Bea sat on the couch with Kilroy rapidly pecking her fingernails. He was chirping and scritching like a small monkey, producing all his sounds in such rapid progression he sounded like a flock of Kilroys.

"Bea," Eleanor said firmly. "You know Donald Eston?"

"Yes." Bea looked at her slyly.

She knew she had to be absolutely clear, for both Bea and Chandra. "Did you know that he has a reputation for hurting little girls?"

Chandra swivelled around and stared at her. Bea seemed bewildered. "What?"

"Donald Eston has maybe hurt other little girls and might hurt Chandra." She turned to the girl. "Has he touched you? Done anything that he's told you not to tell anyone about?"

"No." Chandra's eyes widened with what looked to Eleanor like truth. She examined the girl's face before turning back to Bea. "Bea. Do you understand? Donald Eston might be a bad man. He might want to hurt Chandra. So keep him away from her. Where's her mother, anyway?"

The girl's face closed and she turned back to the TV. Bea's expression became spitefully clear. "In the beer parlour," she said. "Soused to the gills." She considered further. "Maybe sleeping it off or snorting something."

So the rumours were true. "What about her father?" Eleanor asked this *sotto voce*, although she knew Chandra was still listening.

"Long gone," said Bea, matching her tone. "Long gone and good riddance." In the following silence, it seemed as if Bea were reviewing the bleak history of more than one member of her family.

"Remember what I told you now," Eleanor said.

"About what?"

"About Donald Eston. To keep Chandra away from him."

Vagueness had again taken over. Standing so near to her, Eleanor could smell an indistinct, not unpleasantly stuffy odour: second-floor residents were bathed only once a week, if that. The bird warbled cheerfully, grooming himself, bending down to rub the top of his head against Bea's fingers.

Mrs. Brown came in for a moment, her face set with some unknown purpose. She nodded briefly and disappeared, but not before Eleanor made another resolution. Enough was enough. She would see Fern this afternoon. They would go and tell Mrs. Brown everything, hand the whole situation to her on a platter like a dish gone bad and then hope to be rid of it.

"Eleanor. Fern. How nice to see you, come in." Mrs. Brown looked up from a pile of papers and ran a hand abstractedly over her new hairdo, a short shag that suited her.

She had a very messy desk, Eleanor thought, for someone who seemed so efficient. "Do you have a few minutes?"

Fern was fiddling with a plastic bag that contained *Many Rooms* and didn't say anything. Her hair looked more flyaway than usual, and there was a yoghurt stain on her shirt. Irritated with both of them, Eleanor searched fruitlessly for some chitchat and gave up. "We have to talk to you about Chandra, that little girl who's here all the time."

"Oh." Mrs. B. took off her reading glasses. "Has she been bothering anyone?"

"Oh, no," Fern found her voice. "We're not complaining about her, we're worried about her. We think she might be in danger."

"Danger?" Mrs. Brown put her papers aside, and for an instant, Eleanor could see her asking God to give her patience. "From what?"

Eleanor closed the office door. "We have reason to believe that there's a child molester living here."

"Oh, lord." Mrs. Brown touched her forehead with the back of her hand like a silent film heroine. After gazing rather longingly at her papers, she pushed her wheeled office chair back from the desk. "Sadly, it wouldn't be the first time some elderly man went bonkers like that. Who is it you're concerned about?"

"Donald Eston," Eleanor said. "And he was, or at least his daughter accused him of being, an abuser, long before he was elderly." They recounted everything they knew about Eston, and Mrs. Brown listened intently. In the end, she said she would of course look into it, but kept her expression neutral.

Before they left, Fern handed Mrs. Brown the book, her hand unusually steady. "Read it," she said. "See what you think."

Within a couple of days, Mrs. Brown dropped by Eleanor's suite to tell her she'd put a stop to Chandra's visits. "I guess I should have done that earlier, but I thought we were helping both her and Bea. That it couldn't hurt to let the girl eat a decent meal now and then, and I'm sure it did Bea good to have some company. Chandra was quiet and never any trouble, and the residents generally like to see young people here."

"And what about Donald Eston?"

"As far as he goes, I don't know," she said carefully. "The book is horrific. You said Thelma's daughter, Corrine, did some research on him?"

"She was planning to write you a letter. Or write the executive board. You haven't received anything yet, eh?"

"No."

Standing up to leave, Mrs. Brown hesitated, then said, "We can't do anything about him until we see what's what. I have to tell you, unless there's any proof or…" She closed her eyes for a moment. "Even if he'd ever been charged and got off on a technicality, or something. But there seems to be nothing on him at all."

"The daughter committed suicide after she wrote the book."

"Yes." But now Mrs. Brown was preoccupied with her own thoughts. "I know Eston's son, George," she said. "I'm afraid he'd raise holy hell if we tried to kick his father out. He was quite persistent while he was on the waiting list." She hesitated, and then said in a softer voice, "I'd just as soon this were kept quiet for now. In the end, public opinion might force him out, but that could backfire against us — against Pleasant Manor. I'd like to avoid a scandal." She stopped. "I mean, not if he's a real danger, of course, but at least for this next while. I have to talk to the board."

"No." Eleanor said. "I mean, yes, I see. As a matter of fact, we've never told anyone. We didn't think people would believe us, and if they did they wouldn't appreciate us sharing the information."

Mrs. Brown nodded and left. Eleanor closed the door.

Eston continued to live at Pleasant Manor, bland and polite as always. Life settled back to a certain normality. Eleanor told herself he was now Mrs. Brown's responsibility, and began to hope again for simple peace and contentment, enjoying the company of Fern and of course Andrew. She imagined gossiping about herself to Olivia. Just think, she would say. Having a lover at her age.

Then Chandra went missing. Megan, the kitchen aide, told Eleanor and Fern as she was refilling the coffee maker in the lounge. "She disappeared yesterday. Her mom came here looking for her and I said, 'Chandra hasn't shown up for, like, it must be two or three weeks now. She's not supposed to be here by herself anymore.' She got mad at me then," Megan went on, her eyebrow ring raised indignantly. "She said she knew that, what did I take her for? Well, I didn't go, 'Everybody takes you for a drunk and an unfit mother,' but I probably looked it. She left then. I guess she ended up calling the cops."

Eleanor heard the rest of Megan's monologue through a panic that seemed related to nothing but herself. She couldn't breathe; it was as if her body were depriving itself of oxygen to give her something else to occupy her mind. "My God." She forced the words out.

Fern had become absolutely still, the tremor shocked out of her as she watched Megan drift away.

Taking deep breaths now, Eleanor watched Fern turn to her in slow motion and say, "Eston. We put pressure on him by telling. What have we done?"

"What did we not do?" Eleanor said.

They made their way out of the building, automatically going to Fern's place to watch the news on TV. Considering the usual alarm surrounding a missing child, the broadcast seemed strangely muted. No amber alert had been initiated. Brooke did not appear on camera tearfully pleading for her child's life. There were just the bare facts, a school picture of Chandra, and then on to the weather.

Fern stood at her window looking out at Eston's front door.

"What are we doing dithering around here?" Eleanor paced the room. "We have to see Mrs. Brown."

Fern shook her head. "We should watch for Eston."

"And do what? If he shows up on his doorstep there, are you going to run over and accost him?"

"You go and talk to Mrs. Brown. I'm staying here."

There was no point arguing. Back at the Manor, Eleanor saw that the TV in the lounge was turned to the local news now, an unusually large number of coffee drinkers buzzing around in front of it. Bea Armitage passed her in the hallway with Kilroy, then stopped and turned to her. "Something happened," she said. The bird sat on her shoulder as usual, but lean and ready for flight.

"Yes." Eleanor could see a ray of sense trying to shine through.

"Brooke told me. I remember now," Bea said calmly, and took off.

Mrs. Brown looked up distractedly from her desk. "Yes, I know about Chandra," she said. Eleanor hadn't yet uttered a word.

"Do the police know about Donald Eston? Are they aware of him being here, now?" Eleanor was struck by a strange floating sensation. Her words seemed to echo inside her head.

"They are, as a matter of fact. But no complaints have ever been laid against him, by anybody." Mrs. Brown looked scattered. She tucked a wisp of greying hair behind her ear. "There's just that book, which didn't name him, and you know the publisher was careful to designate it as fiction, though I guess they didn't promote it that way. The police can't go in and search his place, just like that." She held up her hand in a *just wait* gesture, got up and closed the door. "But it was Eston's cleaning day yesterday. We took it upon ourselves to search very thoroughly while he was out. We didn't find anything. There's no possible place he could hide even books or magazines. He doesn't own a computer."

"How long has Chandra been missing?" But she knew, of course. Why hadn't she heard about it earlier?

"Brooke came looking for her here yesterday morning. She disappeared in the night. While her mother was passed out, no doubt."

"So she's been gone over a full day," Eleanor said flatly.

"Yes. They have a search party out."

When Eleanor got back to Fern's suite, she was still standing by the window. "He's still here," she said. "I saw him. He went into his place as if nothing has happened."

That evening, Andrew came over to Eleanor's to sit with her and Fern and pick at a microwaved fast-food supper. He looked sorry for himself. Dealing with the two of them was too much for him, Eleanor thought, irritated, let alone having to face the idea of Chandra's disappearance. He went home early.

Dennis came by. Beth had called the police, he said, to ask if they were aware of Donald Eston's daughter and her book. They told her they were. Eleanor said she knew that from Mrs. Brown.

"I'm sorry we didn't do anything earlier," Dennis said. He kept picking at a new growth of beard on his chin, and Eleanor had to stifle the urge to grab his hand away from his face. "You were right to be concerned. It seems to Beth and me it's way too much of a coincidence that a kid who had contact with him is missing."

"You couldn't have done any more about him than anyone else has," Eleanor said.

After Dennis went home, Fern stayed. They did nothing and didn't say much all evening, but kept each other company. Fern was on the point of leaving when someone else knocked on the door. Eleanor went slowly to open it, dread jolting her nerves. A knock at this time of night could only mean bad news. A blonde woman stood there, her face in the shadow cast by the porch light, but Eleanor could see she was smiling. Maybe she was one of the new aides Mrs. Brown had hired.

"Hello, Eleanor. How are you?" She stepped forward.

"Corrine! Good heavens, come in. What on earth have you done with your hair?" Realizing she was being rude, she called, "Fern! It's Corrine."

Fern, shakily pushing back her own hair, looked as flustered as Eleanor felt. "For heaven's sake," she said. "Corrine. We were wondering what happened to you."

"Yes. I guess you must have been. I forgot you might not recognize me in poor light. Blondes," she added, patting her smooth new haircut, "are supposed to have more fun." She came in, accepted a glass of wine. "I was driving home from P.A. and thought I'd stop off and see how you were. I knew you'd still be up. I heard about Chandra."

"Yes." Eleanor let a moment pass, then said bluntly, "We haven't heard from you since that meeting, didn't know if you wrote that letter or what." An unsteady anger began to take hold. And what about Thelma? She hadn't even phoned to offer moral support, and here was her daughter, useless as ever.

"I finally sent it," Corrine said. "Only a couple of weeks ago. I have no excuse, just procrastination. I was so wrapped up in problems of my own, and then Mom taking off and all that..." Her voice petered out.

"Your letter must have come about the same time we first talked to Mrs. Brown," Fern said.

"We thought if we complained about Eston being here, something would be done about him," Eleanor added. "But really, she did nothing except prohibit Chandra from visiting, and now she's gone."

"Eston's still here?"

"Yes. The police haven't even bothered to search his place. Anyway, there's no question of him having taken off with her, it's just... It all might have been planned with someone else. Or I suppose he could have put her somewhere. Or her body," she added, her own voice sounding hollow.

Corrine looked aghast. "Well, of course, I knew something like this was always a possibility. That's why I gave Mom the book to share. I should have..." But Corrine didn't finish that thought. "I think I'll talk to the police about Eston," she said. "Try to make them realize what a threat he is."

"Mrs. Brown talked to the police. When they wouldn't search his place, she and the housekeeping staff did so," Eleanor said. "Unofficially. They didn't find anything. Strangely enough, he doesn't own a computer."

"That doesn't mean a trained officer with a search warrant couldn't find something. At least some pictures or something to prove he could still be a predator." For an instant, she looked like Thelma. Corrine was aging in the sudden way that often hit women in their fifties, Eleanor thought. Her blonde hair seemed only to emphasize it.

"How's your mom doing?" Eleanor asked. "All we've heard from her is the odd postcard, and Fern had one phone call when they got back to Calgary."

"Oh!" Corrine stood up. "Before I forget, I have something for you out in the car. Just a minute." She hurried outside and returned with two gift-wrapped packages. "From Mom," she said. "She and Palmer made a quick trip to a border town down south, and I guess these presents are from Mexico."

Fern unwrapped a jewellery box enamelled in bright red and turquoise. Eleanor's gift was a glass bird full of air bubbles, its thick wings spread in an impossible yet oddly graceful way. "How thoughtful of Thelma," she said politely. "She knows I collect glass." She waved at her shelf of ornaments, her windowsill of vases.

"They're planning now to go to Mexico next winter," Corrine said. "Actually, Mom's been so happy travelling around with Palmer, I can't believe I was so set against it." She stood up to go. "I should hit the road," she said. "Let you two get some sleep."

"We won't be getting much of that for a while," Fern said. Her thin face was pinched with exhaustion, her cheeks hollow.

"Tell Thelma to give us a call," Eleanor said.

In the morning, looking dully out her window at a lovely spring day, for the first time in her life Eleanor thought how peaceful, how painless not existing at all would be. She refused to think "better off dead" outright. She didn't want to go down that path quite yet, but the idea of perpetual nothingness had lost its terror. To be or not to be.

She examined Eston's doorway, recalling Thelma's idea of doing away with him. Maybe they could have done something, used some sort of poison, as Thelma suggested, from foxglove or monkshood. God knew, there were enough poisonous plants around. Some simple thing that might have put his already iffy health over the edge.

She was startled out of her thoughts by an ambulance driving right up to the door she was watching, siren blaring. Two men in white hurried into Donald Eston's suite, then out again with him on a stretcher, reminding her of a film that was being run slightly too fast, an episode of Keystone Kops. She felt foggy from so little sleep, and the scene, highlighted in the morning sun, seemed an extension of a dream she couldn't quite remember.

Over at the Manor she stopped the first person she saw, though it happened to be Bea. "What's happened to Donald Eston?"

"Swallowed something," Bea said, looking unusually sane but not particularly concerned.

When Fern didn't show up for morning coffee, Eleanor knocked on her door. She knew all this was likely making Fern too ill to go out. When she finally appeared, she was not only pale and shaking, but tears were forming canals in the lines of her face. This was something more than worry.

"What on earth's happened?" Eleanor took her hand.

"My pills are gone."

"What? What pills?"

"Olivia's sleeping pills. Gone. The whole bottle."

"Olivia's pills?" Eleanor echoed. "How on earth did you end up with those?"

"I had her handbag with me that day, remember? She kept all her pills in her purse."

"You lost them?" Eleanor was too confused to ask why she had them in the first place.

"I think someone stole them. I'm positive they were in my medicine cabinet." She was shaking so badly she could hardly speak. "A brand new prescription, and I can't even report it, since I stole them myself.

There's nothing I can do." Eleanor couldn't understand why she was so devastated until Fern said, "Someone's stolen my good death."

Eleanor let a few seconds tick by before she said, "Fern. I don't think they'd be any help in the end. If you're helpless you can't take them anyway, and otherwise you continue to hope things will improve and you can't bring yourself to do it." Fern shook her head. "Besides, you can get your own prescription. Do you think that's impossible?"

Fern wiped her eyes. "Yes. I suppose I can. I just don't like the idea of asking Doctor Van Deusen, I feel somehow that he'd know. I…my mind isn't well, Eleanor. I've focused so obsessively on those particular Halcions. I thought of them as a gift from Olivia. I don't know what's wrong with me."

"You're depressed. And no wonder." Eleanor thought of the ambulance she'd seen that morning. Of course. "I bet I know who took them."

"What? Who?"

"Donald Eston was taken to the hospital this morning. I guess he swallowed something, tried to kill himself. I bet he's been through other medicine cabinets too, just seeing what he could find."

"Good lord." Fern had to sit down.

Eleanor was afraid Fern was going to faint and sat beside her on the couch. "Put your head down," she said, but Fern ignored her.

"To think of him in here. He could easily have walked in. I often don't lock the door when I'm just over at the Manor."

They decided to look for the pills in case she'd absentmindedly set them somewhere, forgotten that she hadn't put them away. Dumping the contents of her purse on the bedspread, they combed through everything, the loose Kleenexes, the extra change, the face powder compact. Fern looked under the couch, bending stiffly on her knees, holding a weak flashlight. "Lord. I thought this was vacuumed only last week," she said.

"Pockets," Eleanor suggested. "Look through all your pockets." But they found nothing.

"Let's go for a walk," Fern said. "I can't stand just sitting here. If Eston has tried to kill himself, what happened to that poor child? What on earth is going on? Sometimes I wish I'd taken those pills as soon as I got hold of them."

Eleanor ignored this. Once outside in the neighbourhood, she looked up at the canopy of elm trees sheltering the street, the leaves rustling. In spite of all this misery she was grateful it wasn't winter. "Do you know that poem, is it by Whitman? About a tree uttering leaves?"

Fern wasn't ready to be distracted. "I guess if he took them I can't do much about it. I might as well make an appointment to see Dr. Van Deusen about getting some of my own. I don't like to though."

"Oh, the doctor's always so busy he won't suspect anything," Eleanor said. "He'll be happy to prescribe something just to get rid of you." She stopped walking for a moment, realizing what she was encouraging Fern to do.

Dennis phoned. He had talked to the Mounties in P.A., he said, to someone he knew there. "I told him my mother was a friend of Chandra's grandmother's, and that we all wanted to know why they hadn't used the amber alert. The guy — he's a corporal — said they had a lead. He told me, in so many words, to mind my own business."

Eleanor was grateful for his efforts and said so. "There's nothing much more anyone can do until the police let the public know what's happening. I'll let you know if we hear anything."

It was late in the evening and Andrew had joined Eleanor at Fern's place. She told them what Dennis had said. They sat for a long while, the TV on the news channel on mute, showing the subtitles for the deaf. Chandra had made the news for one day. One day only and then that was it. "You know what we need?" Andrew said.

"What?" Fern was gazing bleakly at one of her spider plants.

"A drink."

"Yes." Fern looked surprised, relieved, as if this were an unusual, particularly enticing, idea. Eleanor knew she still had a good couple of bottles of gin stashed in her china cabinet.

They were on their fourth gin and tonic before Eleanor felt numb enough to discuss Eston again. "I just can't fathom what goes on in his mind. If he's tried to kill himself, it must mean he has feelings, can be overcome with despair."

"Just think how he's feeling if he's not guilty," Andrew said.

"Would someone who is guilty of all that *have* feelings?" Fern asked. "He certainly seems to be affected by things directly to do with him, with himself."

Was that what it was like, Eleanor wondered? People capable of such atrocities had feelings only for themselves? No idea what compassion was, no sense of affinity with other beings? She was reminded of recent headlines. "Did you hear on the news again about those child porn websites on the internet?" she asked.

"Oh lord." Fern said, "I've had enough of all this. Let's have another drink and just watch a talk show."

It was two o'clock in the morning when Eleanor covered Fern with a blanket on her couch and staggered, holding on to Andrew's chair, across the street to her own place. Andrew was fully able to wheel himself back to his own suite. A bit too used to lots of alcohol, she caught herself thinking as her bedroom whirled around her.

In the morning, weakened by nausea and the ache splitting her head, so unsteady she couldn't make coffee, Eleanor wondered how anyone could think booze was the answer to anything. There was nothing more miserable than a hangover. She swallowed Aspirin and Gravol and returned to bed, a cold cloth on her forehead, to wait it out.

In the afternoon, after some dry toast with coffee, she sat at the table by the window, noting that the ash trees, so slow to bud, were finally in full leaf. She wondered how Fern was doing. She saw Eston's son come out of his place carrying boxes of paper recycling and assorted junk. He must be there cleaning up. As she watched him plod back inside, she felt sorry for him.

She set down her cup. If anybody knew something, you'd think this man would. About his father's past, if not about Chandra. She should watch for his next visit, drop in on him when she felt better. But her lightheadedness led to a feeling of recklessness. She found herself standing up, closing her door behind her, and crossing the street without her cane. She rang Eston's doorbell.

The son stood warily in the doorway. "Yes?"

"Mr. Eston? My name is Eleanor Sawchuck. I need to talk to you."

He looked alarmed, taken aback. "Yes?" he repeated.

"I know your father and his circumstances. I want to find some things out from you." She saw he was about to refuse. "Please," she said, feeling suddenly faint. She put her hand on the door frame. "I need to sit down." He shook his head and took her arm, silently led her into the kitchen and seated her on a vinyl-cushioned chair. "Thank you." She must look like hell, she realized. She must look a hundred years old.

He sat across from her at the table, not offering anything. He was a florid man, rather jowly, as if he'd been fat at one time and lost weight. He plucked nervously at a flap of skin under his chin.

"You may think I'm impertinent and intrusive, but something like this should be everyone's business," Eleanor said. She knew she sounded officious, had the weird thought that she was channelling Olivia, but at least she was able to talk. "I have two questions." He was about to stand up and she put her hand out to stop him. "I want to know if your sister's book is true. That's the first and obvious question." She felt stronger now, running on adrenaline. "And more important at this late date, has your father had anything to do with Chandra Armitage's disappearance?"

He sat back down. He looked sicker than she felt now, and angry. She wondered if she were safe.

"Who are you?" he asked, his voice raspy. "To push yourself in here?"

"You have a father who's been accused by your own sister of sexual abuse, of torturing her as a child. I have reason to believe he may still be a predator, and you're asking why? I've had to live as his neighbour, knowing all this, and now I want to know the truth."

"The truth? Do you think if I knew without a doubt, that I would have anything to do with him?"

Recalling something she'd read once about the loyalty of children of Nazi war criminals, she remained silent. He rubbed his face with one hand, as if washing it of something.

"I'm not long for this world, Mr. Eston." The cliché had escaped her mouth before she could stifle it.

He gave her a brief glance. "I can see that," he said bluntly.

"I've tried to come to terms with living near him," Eleanor said. "Someone gave that book to me to read before he moved here. If I'd have known I'd be meeting him, I likely wouldn't have read it, but since I did, I have to know. If you can tell me your real opinion...." She glanced at him. He was looking down at the floor, shaking his head. "It would bring me some peace to know what you think, either way."

He wouldn't look at her. "Okay. Fine. This isn't going to help you any, but this is what I know." He seemed to be watching something just past her shoulder. "I'm not sure why my mother consented to this, but when my parents split up, she left Iris with my father out at the acreage. She took me to Calgary. I was a baby. All I can recall of my dad in those years of growing up is his visiting me in the city, once in a while, taking me on outings. Iris would be with him. That's all. I didn't sense anything, didn't notice a thing. Iris was always weird. When her book came out, I stood behind my father." He rubbed his face again.

She watched him. His attitude had softened; he seemed almost relieved. "You never saw anything suspicious? That made you wonder?"

"I asked my mother why Iris never came to visit. Why I never went there to stay. All she said was that she couldn't handle her, and my father didn't like her to leave home, it always upset her. Later I found out she was afraid Iris might hurt me. Iris never said anything about anything, but she was five years older and she resented me. Hated me. I could tell that much. I was afraid of her as a child, and I simply never saw her after we grew up. She wouldn't see me or my mother, and of course not him. After the book came out I... He swore every word of it is a lie. And how could you believe that kind of thing about your own father? I still can't."

"What did your mother think?"

"She denied it could have happened. Well, we never referred to that book except right after it came out. She said then that Iris was always horrible to her, couldn't be trusted around me, was totally unmanageable whenever she saw her. She thought that book was proof Iris was disturbed."

Eleanor had almost heard enough to know she was no further ahead than before she'd made this effort. She prepared to get up and leave. She really didn't feel well.

"But then in the end," he said, "when my mother's mind was foggy, kind of weak but not senile," he hesitated, glanced at Eleanor, "she started talking about it. She'd had suspicions she wouldn't acknowledge even to herself and now thought the book provided answers to questions she'd refused to ask. But then another time she said again it was all made up. Once, when she was clearer than usual, she said maybe a fraction of it had actually happened, but she had long ago refused to believe any of it. If she had, her life would have been hell."

Eleanor nodded. "So."

"At any rate, after my mom died I began to look after him. His health wasn't good. He felt persecuted, and it was true, people found out where he lived in Edmonton and were harassing him. It died down for a while, but then there was a reprint and suddenly it was being talked about again. A new crop of women read it. Eventually I moved him out here, where I could keep an eye on him. I won't allow him a computer. I told him it wouldn't look good." He folded his hands on the table. Eleanor could see his knuckles were white. "Right from the beginning, my wife wouldn't let him near our daughters. Nothing was ever said, but that's how it was."

"They were born after the book came out?"

"They were babies."

"This must be terrible for all of you."

He seemed too distracted to acknowledge her sympathy. "One day after he'd been here in Kasokinaw for some time, we passed Bea Armitage with that little girl and they stopped, chatted with him like old friends. Chandra said thank you for the present. I took him back here and gave him hell. What did he think he was doing? He said he was lonely. For Christ's sake." His words now were barely audible. Then something else seemed to strike him. He raised his head to look her straight in the eye.

Now what? she wondered, but he said nothing. Then it occurred to her: he must recall that note of Thelma's. She looked back at him.

The note wasn't hers, and even if it had been, she would not be intimidated.

He said nothing now for such a long time that Eleanor said, "And so?"

He stood up, not looking at her at all now. "And so, that's all I have." He hesitated, a furtive shadow clouding his face for a second. "No idea at all about Chandra Armitage, except that he had nothing to do with her disappearance. He's in no shape to do anything." He glanced at Eleanor as if he could say the same about her. "Do you need help getting home?"

"No. I came here under my own power and I can walk the few yards back." As she stood to go, she sensed he was holding something back, but she didn't feel well enough to ask anything more. She told him she hoped to see him again.

14

She was pursuing someone, a vague shape-shifting figure, down a back alley overgrown on each side by lilac bushes. Pushing branches and heavy purple blooms aside, she found herself passing Chandra's backyard, where she could barely perceive the form of a child. But it wasn't Chandra, she realized, it was the mother, Brooke. In the surreal logic of the dream, she was abruptly transferred to Palmer's niece's house, mildly surprised to find a baby in the centre of the bed. When Eleanor woke up, she was overwhelmed by another idea and decided she had to act before she thought twice about it. She told herself she had to keep trying. Otherwise she might as well throw in her cards and hope for, if not death, simple memory loss.

"I think I'll try to talk to Chandra's mother," she told Fern and Andrew. "She lives just a couple of blocks from here."

"Eleanor, she's an alcoholic," Fern said. "And with her daughter missing, you can't just … you'll get in over your head. I still can't believe you went over to Eston's place and talked to his son."

"If you insist on going," Andrew said, "I'll go with you."

She knew Andrew didn't approve of her interfering, thought that any visiting she did would end badly. Not dangerously, but in some sort of scene, something he would prefer to avoid at all costs. "I don't need anyone with me," she said. "Nobody's going to do anything to an old lady dropping by to extend sympathy. And she may talk to me if I'm by myself."

Andrew's chair was pulled up beside one of the ornate benches, where Eleanor sat leaning back against the wrought iron. For a few minutes she refused to dwell on anything but the sun warming her and illuminating the front façade of the old Manor. She thought how absurd the concrete image of the Virgin Mary looked guarding automated glass doors. Mary's face had become as worn and pockmarked as the faded red brick surrounding it, and Eleanor wondered how, after a century of Saskatchewan weather, it managed to retain its complacent expression.

Halfway to Brooke's house, her determination faltered, and she wondered what she was doing. Did she think she was Miss Marple? But she persuaded herself to pass by a cottage garden on Brooke's block that she and Andrew would sometimes stop to admire. Basket-of-gold flowers shone piercing yellow against blue forget-me-nots. Bushy peony plants showed knots of hard green buds waiting for summer.

She continued on, drawn toward Brooke's backyard as she'd been in the dream. Her stomach knotted when she realized that yes, there was a young woman sitting on the steps, looking half awake, in a baggy T-shirt and sweat shorts. What were the odds? Then again, why wouldn't someone be sitting on their back steps with a mug of coffee on a beautiful day in June?

Eleanor told herself she was merely an old lady going for a walk. She could pass by, maybe smile and nod and say what a lovely day. She stopped. She walked into the yard where there was in fact a lilac bush, weedy and neglected, showing a couple of pale buds. "Brooke Armitage?"

The woman looked up, surprised. "Yeah?" Her hair, brown streaked with platinum, hung in strings, and acne dotted her forehead. A steel stud pierced the crease between her bottom lip and chin. With her full lips, straight nose and cool green eyes, she would have been beautiful if her face hadn't been swollen with drugs or sleep. Or maybe she was just too fat. The T-shirt didn't show much of her figure. Eleanor gazed at her a bit too long, trying to see a resemblance to Chandra. "Well, what?" Brooke asked, half standing.

"I'm Eleanor Sawchuck, from Pleasant Manor? I, uh, I knew your little girl from when she used to visit."

If she expected Brooke's face to crumple, she was mistaken. "So?" Her tone was insolently defensive, like a moody teenager's.

Contempt rose in Eleanor's throat. How old was this woman? Twenty-six? Seven? "I'm sorry. I just wanted to say how sorry I am for," she stumbled, about to say for your loss, but that implied death.

"Don't be." But Brooke's expression weakened. Eleanor knew that look, from dealing with her brother. The addict's abiding core of self-pity, showing through. That whiny appreciation for being noticed with sympathy.

"Don't be?" Eleanor couldn't help repeating. She caught a whiff of the alcohol in Brooke's cup now and was almost overcome by a hopelessness that sapped her strength.

"Here." The girl shoved herself over to one side. "Have a seat, you look a bit peaked."

Peak-id. Such an old-fashioned idiom. Eleanor sat.

"You're wondering how I can be so cool about Chandra missing." Her speech wasn't slurred at all.

"Yes. I guess so." Eleanor felt almost as if she'd had a spell of some kind. Or had a spell cast on her.

"The thing is…" the girl stopped, gave her a sly look that made Eleanor want to slap her. "I know where she is," she said simply, and shrugged. She lit a cigarette, inhaled deeply.

Eleanor had to search for her voice. "What?"

"She's with Phil, her dad. My ex."

Stunned, Eleanor couldn't say a thing.

"He just came and got her. Let me worry for a day until he phoned, said he'd kill me if I told the cops it was him. He let me talk to her." She looked down at her bitten nails, then glanced again at Eleanor. "Don't think you're anyone special," she said. "I've told tons of people, except the cops, and nobody's said anything. Isn't that funny? In this shit-hole, the gossip capital of the universe, nobody's said anything because they figure Chandra's better off with an ex-con with no fixed address than she was with me. Just because he was the pharmacist's son."

The pharmacist. Yes. The town's previous pharmacist and his wife. Were they dead too? She didn't think she could bear knowing they had retired to a warm climate, leaving Chandra to her feckless parents. "The Lawsons?" she asked. They would now be sixty or so.

"Yes. Lawsons. They said if I was stupid enough to have the baby, they'd have nothing to do with us." She picked at a hangnail. "They tried to cover all their bases, saying the baby wasn't Phil's anyway."

"Where are they now?"

"Who knows? They split up a few years ago."

"How could the police not know that Phil has Chandra? Are they that stupid?"

"I bet they do know, just not officially." Her tone was bitter. "Because they think the same as everybody else." She sat up, straightening her shoulders. "If you want to know the truth," she said, becoming momentarily sensible, confiding, "They're right. She is better off with Phil."

Eleanor shook her head, not in disagreement, but in dismay at such evidence of waste. She could see Brooke's future in the intense way her hands cradled her drink. She was past finding incentive to change. Just as it had been for Tom, Brooke's existence didn't revolve around her addiction, it was her addiction. She could love nothing else.

"What is Phil like?" Eleanor asked her. "Does he work?"

"He works construction, off and on, under the table. Maybe with a kid to look after he'll finally have to stay in one place. He won't like that though. He's still...he makes money selling dope."

"Oh."

"Just marijuana," Brooke assured her. "He stuck around, you know, after Chandra was born. He was a pretty good dad, as far as that goes." For a split second her face took on a harsh grimace. "Until he left her."

They sat there for some time, rather companionably. Eleanor knew she should go. "But why did he choose now to show up like that?" she asked.

"Somebody called him about that old guy in Pleasant Manor. Said did he realize Chandra was vulnerable to a child molester. That set him in motion, all right." Her voice contained a note of satisfaction.

Why didn't it set you in motion? Eleanor thought. "Weren't you concerned about him?" she asked, keeping own her voice deadpan, polite. "The old guy, I mean."

"Naw." Brooke looked off into space. "He's just a harmless geezer."

How did she know what he was? That she knew him at all made Eleanor suspect he'd been around courting her as well as Bea. Maybe buying booze for her. Who could have phoned Chandra's father? If Fern had done anything, she would have said. Corrine? Thelma?

"Anyway, some guy called, out of the blue. Somehow tracked down Phil's cell number."

"His *cell* number?" Eleanor asked, but then felt immediately foolish.

Brooke's eyes became greener with disdain. "Cell phone number. And so Phil started thinking what he could do." She got up for a moment, staggered and sat down again.

This evidence of drunkenness forced Eleanor to her feet. "I just hope Chandra's all right." Gripping her cane, she watched the young woman for a sign she could be believed. Brooke sat absently winding a lock of hair around her finger, and Eleanor glimpsed something of Bea in her blemished face.

She limped through the yard past a rusted patio table brushed by a stand of foxtails. She stopped near the straggly lilac bush at the entrance. "Thank you for telling me," she said. Brooke nodded, taking a careful sip from her cup.

Eleanor knew from Thelma that Brooke had been fourteen when she started drinking, and she'd read somewhere that alcoholics and addicts remained emotionally at the age they were when they first became addicted. She recognized this as the truth.

Then again, Chandra seemed to show no signs of fetal alcohol syndrome. Maybe Brooke had cared enough, had managed to quit drinking while she was pregnant. And since she'd been living with the father, maybe Social Services had given her the benefit of the doubt, hadn't taken much trouble over Chandra at the time. Maybe they never knew about her in the first place. Who would have notified them? Now the community, by keeping its maw of a mouth shut for a change, was complicit in Chandra's escape. If that's what you could call it.

She was surprised to hear it was a man who'd called Chandra's father, and was still mulling this over when she met up with Fern and Andrew and told them what happened. "Was it you?" she asked Andrew.

"No. It wasn't me." He said this in a near whisper. Surprise and relief seemed to have robbed him of his voice.

She called Dennis, and told him the news. "You weren't the one who called Phil, were you?"

"God, no. I might have if I'd have thought of it."

"Maybe it was Eston's son," Fern said. "Didn't you say you thought he was holding something back?"

"Yes." She recalled him at the end of her visit, about to say something and thinking better of it.

At least Chandra was safe from Donald Eston. Of course, now he was in the hospital anyway. Maybe with any luck he'd pass quietly away. She worried about the fact that no one had notified the police officially, since expensive resources were being wasted. Or were they? According to Brooke, the police weren't bothering anymore. And what about Chandra's father, who would probably go to jail if the cops did find him?

Later that evening, Andrew arrived with a bottle of brandy in the side pocket of his wheelchair. "We need something medicinal," he said. "And celebratory."

"Andrew. We've just recovered from our last bender."

"I'm not proposing a bender. Just a drink. You were right, Eleanor, to insist on talking to Brooke. At least we know the girl's alive and well, and maybe now we ourselves can start living again." He gave her a tentative look, which she wasn't yet in the mood to acknowledge.

"Yes," Fern said. "We do need to celebrate." She accepted the bottle. "We can mix ours with soda," she assured Eleanor.

The brandy and soda went down so easily, Eleanor was pouring herself a third before she knew it. "You too?" she asked, waving the bottle.

"I'm not supposed to, but what the hell," Fern said.

"You only live once." Eleanor poured two stiff ones. Andrew was about to pour himself another snifter when he abruptly set the bottle back down on the table. "I have to admit," he said, "I'm not the drinker

I once was. I think I'd better go home and get some sleep." Eleanor was about to leave with him, but was right then so comfortable she found it impossible to move. By the time she made a small effort to get up, he'd wheeled himself out the door.

Fingering the rim of her crystal glass, Fern continued to watch the door after Andrew's departure. "You know," she started to say, then stopped. The glass glowed amber, her earrings sparkled in the lamplight. "I always envied you and Olivia. Marriage, kids, immersed in the whole mess while I watched from the sidelines. And here you are again."

"Fern. You didn't sit on any sidelines and you know it." She held her own glass up to the light. Though it still showed half full, she felt so good she thought she would risk pouring herself a fourth. "And how can you say forty years of teaching school was avoiding mess? Or anything?" She was reminded of Olivia's affair. "Did Olivia ever tell you?" she asked and then stopped. She put her glass down carefully. She'd always known she would end up telling Olivia's secret to Fern. "About an affair she had?"

"Oh, yes. Harvey Malloy."

"You mean you knew! She told you about it?" Astonished jealousy caused her to forget everything else for the moment.

"No. Well, not exactly. I just knew Olivia so well. I saw her more often in those years than you did, remember, because I was teaching in Poplar Bluff."

Eleanor tried to recall that time, Olivia and Zack moving to Mont Herbert. It wasn't that far from Kasokinaw, but they'd been busy, and she and Olivia had seen each other only every few weeks, usually when Fern picked them up for trips to Prince Albert. "You could have said something," Eleanor said, "even if you were only suspicious."

"She never told me anything," Fern said. "And I just didn't feel like gossiping about Olivia like that behind her back. Even to you." They sat silently. "Sex," Fern continued. "Well, of course I never found the right person. Then again, maybe Olivia didn't either, at least to marry."

When Fern was young, she'd possessed a peculiar, subtle beauty that wasn't immediately evident. Men were always falling for her after it was too late, Eleanor recalled. Once she became friendly and comfortable with someone, Fern told her, the attraction wore off. She was always having crushes on new people and being initially ignored, then courted unsuccessfully after they got to know her. "How can a couple live together for years and still want to make love?" she asked Eleanor once. "Familiarity breeds contempt if you're not compatible and a sibling-like comfort if you are."

"It comes and goes," Eleanor told her. "You have to give it time. Years, I mean." They'd been in their thirties by then, set in their lives, and knew Fern would likely remain in single bliss, as she called it.

Now she said, "I've always thought, Fern, you never gave anybody a chance. You have to wait out the down times."

"It seems to me living with any man would be one big down time. If I'd have been raised nowadays I might have tried." She stopped. "Well, something else."

Eleanor carefully lifted the soda bottle off the coffee table. "We might as well finish the soda water. We'll feel better later." She had always known Fern was attracted to both sexes, but it was nothing they ever talked about, and Eleanor wouldn't encourage her now. They'd known each other too long. Airing such ancient knowledge could cause disintegration of some kind.

Eleanor glanced down at her knee, grimly aware of how old she and Fern were. Nothing could bring their lives back. The choices they made in the past were now carved in stone. Watching the fizz die in her soda water, she wondered if she'd missed her one chance on this earth for rapture. Maybe she should have tried to seduce Max, all those years ago. She closed her eyes, but the darkness made her slightly dizzy. She took a long drink of water. Of course, the very idea was stupid. She'd been too young; Max thought of her as a child. But later. After she was already married to Orest.

Fern was examining her glass too, holding it against the light. "God knows how that brandy interacted with my medication."

Since Fern knew about Olivia, Eleanor thought, and since she knew about Fern, she wondered if either of them ever had any idea about her crush on her father-in-law. Well, how could they? Aside from that one drunken New Year's kiss, which she was convinced nobody, including Max himself, remembered, she hadn't done anything about it.

"You know, it's funny," Fern said. Eleanor gave a start; she felt as if she'd been asleep. They each took another drink of soda water.

"What's funny?"

"That Mrs. Brown never saw fit to do anything about Donald Eston."

"Yes." Eleanor didn't mind the change of subject.

"After Chandra went missing, I, well, I contemplated just getting rid of him. I thought, if a child goes missing in the vicinity of a child molester, what are the odds? I just, I convinced myself he had to be guilty, and that now he had struck again." She grimaced. "Struck again. Like some comic-book bad guy. I started planning, and then one day I realized it was all impossible. I couldn't kill anyone, even if I had absolute proof." She looked off into space, as if she saw there something vaguely amusing. "And then of course he tried to kill himself anyway."

"If it was his son who phoned Chandra's father," Eleanor said, "I think that's pretty damning evidence."

"Yes," Fern agreed. "If his own son is going to those lengths to protect someone from him, I would think at least part of what that girl wrote is true."

"At times I've been able to talk myself into believing he could be innocent," Eleanor said, "Sort of like Orest was with religion. You know, he was a non-believer, but after he became ill he went about converting himself. He said the concept of the complete annihilation of his whole being was insupportable. Inconceivable, really."

Fern looked stricken, and Eleanor was sorry to have brought death into the conversation. "Did he succeed?" Fern asked.

"I don't think he had enough time. But I don't know." Eleanor considered how alone everyone is at the end. What a tragedy that was. Or was it? Maybe it was just the brandy, but at that moment she felt grounded in certainty, of what she wasn't quite sure. Herself, somehow. Still, she went on, "It's strange I haven't been thinking all that much about my own death. I guess I don't feel it staring me personally in the face just yet."

They were both suddenly so tired, they couldn't keep their eyes open. Fern finished her soda and went home.

15

It wasn't that Eleanor was a blessing counter, but back in winter she'd been surprised to find how quickly she became used to Andrew's wheelchair. And now, though he refused therapy, he was becoming stronger on his own. He could stand and walk a little, managed well enough so he was in no danger of having to move to the second floor. On their outings to Nancy's house, Andrew sometimes exercised by taking a turn pushing her in the chair.

Even after all they'd been through, they still couldn't get enough of each other. She thought of those years in Prince Albert alone in her own house after Orest died, when she'd come to rely on small pleasures: her garden, her coffee in the morning, a good book, visits with Fern and Olivia or her family, a letter from one of her grandchildren. She'd always told herself she found joy most potent in miniature, in memories of small moments. Orest, sheepish and joking, bringing her a present from town. A teasing, ordinary kiss from Dennis when he was little.

In Prince Albert she'd still had her car, she could shop for herself, she could go places. Even when she didn't want to leave home, the possibility had been there, the freedom to choose, and she'd chosen peace and solitude.

But this. Andrew. He was a gift, an unexpected dessert just as she was preparing to leave the banquet. Her just dessert. She looked down and noted, not for the first time, how muscular his arms had become since his accident.

Glancing back at her, Andrew asked, "And what are you smiling at?"

"At you," she said. She let go of the handles to walk beside him for awhile, let him wheel himself over a smooth section of sidewalk.

Now, after several months, though she and Andrew still went over to the house every few days, they sometimes didn't have ordinary sex at all. But they made love. It was the touching, the intimacy that was important.

Dennis's face took on a peculiar shade whenever he saw them together. She didn't know which was worse, that tamped-down incredulity or the condescending amusement of some of the staff at Pleasant Manor. The reaction from the people her own age ranged from prudish condemnation to sly envy to good-humoured applause to simple acceptance. She couldn't afford to care about any of it.

Eleanor found the spring warmth energizing, and they were moving as hastily as they could. Although he never mentioned it, she knew Andrew had refilled his Viagra prescription. She thought of the nightgown she had packed in her purse and had a brief urge to take it out and stroke the material. No matter how much you were in love, at her age complete nudity wasn't the way to go. Besides, she loved how her breasts felt, encased in silk. An image crossed her mind, of Orest watching her with an unidentifiable look on his face.

She stopped for a moment and waved her hand to clear off a cloud of harmless mosquitoes. "Those are the males." Andrew glanced at her, grinning. "They exist on sap from plants. It's the females that need blood."

"Yes, dear. I know." They continued on their way.

She and Andrew had closed out all except very good friends from their lives. Andrew still played pool with a couple of his old buddies, and Fern sometimes joined the two of them for Scrabble games and Sunday dinners. Eleanor made sure she and Fern continued to visit and go for walks together. Still, she felt guilty. She knew Fern wasn't happy or healthy and that she was letting her down. But she felt strong and vital, pushing Andrew's chair in the early summer sunshine. She felt well. She couldn't worry about everyone, all the time.

Andrew was peering into the distance. "My vision's gone a bit wonky again," he said. She stopped, bending to look at him. He closed one eye like Popeye. "I can't see properly out of my right eye."

"What do you mean, *again?*" He'd never mentioned this before.

"No. No, it's better now." He blinked rapidly. "Comes and goes."

Eleanor hesitated. "Maybe you should…" She didn't know what.

"Don't be daft, my girl. I mentioned it before I thought. It's nothing. Here, you sit now, I'll push."

"No it's still my turn. I need the exercise, too, you know."

"You'll have enough exercise today, my love, to last a lifetime."

"Oh, you," she said.

Late that afternoon, as Eleanor lay in bed with her head on Andrew's shoulder, she felt him fall, not asleep, but into something else that seemed farther down into unconsciousness. His breathing wasn't right. "Andrew!" She patted his face until he opened his eyes, looking up at her, disoriented.

"I must have dozed off," he said. She decided not to mention her concern until later. Right now she'd better concentrate on getting him back to the Manor.

Sitting across from him in the kitchen, she called to see if Murray could pick them up, and Andrew didn't object. The effort of getting dressed had left him pale and exhausted. "My last true love," he said, looking at her so intently she looked down, tracing the pattern of the table. She lifted his hand to her face, rubbing her cheek against it like a cat.

"There's something wrong with me, Eleanor," he said calmly.

She let go of his hand. "I thought so! I thought you weren't just sleeping there. We'll go straight home and have Mrs. Brown take a look at you."

"I think I've had some sort of…" He cleared his throat. "I can't feel the right side of myself properly. Look at my face." She peered at him as if he were some distance away, and stifled a spark of hysteria. "Does it seem normal to you?" He spoke clearly enough, but out of just the one side of his mouth.

"Chrétien," she said, panic rising to her throat.

"I beg your pardon?"

"You're speaking like Jean Chrétien."

"The bloody hell I am," he said, sounding so insulted, she leaned back from the table and laughed. For a moment, hysteria took over and he watched her with the uxorious smile of a man whose wife appreciates his jokes. She gained control, knowing she should call an ambulance. She'd just picked up the phone when Murray showed up. After she answered his terse rap on the back door, he took one look at both of them and said, "I'll drive you to the hospital." She'd forgotten she'd called him. He was like a burly superhero, showing up unannounced to save the day.

Andrew was asleep when she left him. The doctor told Eleanor to go home, they'd do some tests, but it was surely a stroke and they'd have to wait and see. On the drive back to Kasokinaw, Murray was silent as usual, but she could feel his sympathy. Lights from oncoming cars seemed too bright, as if they were warning of something. Soon they'd turn off the main highway and drive the rest of the way home on alternating patches of gravel and crumbling asphalt, but in welcome darkness. Overhead was the gibbous spring moon. Gibbous was the word, wasn't it? Yes: not quite full, not all there. Humpbacked.

Although Murray didn't have his earphones on, she noticed them sticking out of his shirt pocket. "What kind of music do you listen to?" she asked.

"Oh, lots of stuff. Rock and roll, country, blues, Some jazz, even classical. Everything except pop."

"Just like my son." She leaned back in the seat and closed her eyes. She had better phone Dennis, she thought.

But once she was home she was too tired and upset to talk to anyone but Fern.

"Have you called his son in Vancouver?" Fern asked.

"Andrew called him himself."

"It can't be that bad then, can it?"

"No, it didn't seem that bad."

"Have you eaten anything?"

"No." Eleanor realized she'd forgotten about food.

Fern went over to the Manor for a plate of supper leftovers and settled in with Eleanor for the evening. She wasn't shaking at all, but she didn't seem lethargic, either, and Eleanor wondered briefly if she was on something new. "Did the doctors give you anything?" Fern asked. "Just to help you cope for tonight? Or any help at all?"

"No." Eleanor picked at an ice-cream scoop of mashed potatoes.

"There's no excuse for that. They just don't care about people any more. Tommy Douglas must be spinning in his grave."

She patted Fern's hand. "Don't worry about me. It wasn't the doctor's fault; I didn't ask anyone for anything."

"Maybe you should go to bed, try to get some sleep," Fern said. This evening she was like her younger self, strong and reassuring.

"I'll just sit here awhile."

"I'll leave you one of my new sleeping pills." Fern had managed to get the doctor to give her a prescription. She found an egg cup in the cupboard and dropped in a couple of the tiny white tablets.

Eleanor had nightmares so realistic she remained in a fog long after she got up the next morning. She remembered one of the dreams with particular clarity. Max was sitting across the kitchen table, telling her something in Ukrainian. He seemed to expect her to understand, and when she couldn't, became more and more agitated until he lunged at her, breaking the glass she was holding. She ran outside into snow that seemed like quicksand, bogging her down, making it impossible for her to move. She woke up shivering.

She described her nightmare to Fern, as if that might get rid of it. "It took me quite a while to realize Orest's dad wasn't after me. It seems now more like a hallucination than a dream."

"Those pills." Fern was dismayed. "I'm sorry."

"It certainly wasn't your fault," Eleanor said. "I did get some sleep, after all. Have you tried them?"

"No. I'm saving them all in case I ever really need them."

Eleanor didn't want to consider any of this, so didn't comment.

"Do you think you're up to going to the hospital today?" Fern asked.

"I'm going whether I'm up to it or not."

"I'll go with you then."

"You don't have to. I'd appreciate it, but you know I can manage on my own. Andrew's son is coming in from Vancouver. I guess he'll have to handle things by himself for now; his sister lives in Australia and has some complicated arrangements to make."

Fern held a steady hand over the table. "I've had a couple of good days in a row without feeling so tired. I'd better take advantage of it while I can be of some use to somebody."

Fern was rallying her strength to be a support to her. Eleanor was moved and grateful, and began to cry.

"He'll be all right." Fern tried to comfort her. "He was able to talk and move around, wasn't he? He can still get by. You two can still manage."

As Eleanor busied herself making more coffee, she glanced out the side window and saw Mrs. Brown hesitating on her doorstep, taking a deep breath before knocking. "Fern." She felt her voice rise. "It's Mrs. Brown. She has bad news." When Fern opened the door, Eleanor stood behind her. "He's dead, isn't he?"

"No." Mrs. Brown came inside and put her hand on her shoulder. "But he's had another stroke, this one massive, and he's not expected to survive."

She had a sensation of being caught in an elevator, falling. Mrs. Brown helped her to the bathroom, and she emerged emptied of more than her breakfast. She could float away into nothing, she thought, if she let herself go. "I'll be all right," she said to Mrs. Brown. "You have other things to do, and Fern is here."

"Do you remember that poem by Emily Brontë?" asked Eleanor.

"Which one?"

"The one about grief. How she wades in grief and if there's something of a respite, she loses her balance."

"That's Dickinson," Fern said.

Eleanor searched for a Kleenex. "What?"

"It's by Emily Dickinson, not Emily Brontë."

"Yes. That's right." But at any rate, it wasn't appropriate. Her own loss of balance was because of more grief, not because of any respite.

Andrew's son phoned Mrs. Brown to request there be no visitors until he was stabilized. "His son doesn't know how important you are," Fern told Eleanor. "Give him a day or so and then we'll just go up and see him."

Eleanor paced the hallway at the Manor until she was exhausted. Not many people spoke to her about Andrew, but Bea Armitage eyed her briefly and said, "Too much for him, were you?" Eleanor had a quick image of herself sneaking to Bea's room in the middle of the night, pushing a pillow hard onto her face.

She rested on the bench by the plants, looking out at the grey sidewalk and rain-swollen clouds. All those early months wasted, she thought. She should have set her cap at Andrew as soon as she realized she liked him, just as she'd done over sixty years ago with Orest. But of course, how could she? She examined the ghostly reflection the grey day allowed her to see in the glass doors. At her age, how was she to know she could set her cap at anyone? And of course she should be grateful, she was grateful, for the months they did have.

Dread began to weigh on her like a heavy coat. What would someone be like after a massive stroke? At least it shouldn't be painful, not like cancer or heart. She didn't feel all that well herself. She briefly considered the idea that maybe she could put off her visit.

16

Eleanor didn't know what she should have prepared for, but it wasn't this. When Andrew first saw her walk into his hospital room, he gave a great moan, a howl resonating with despair and desperation. He wasn't able to form words, he could move nothing but his eyes, which glared at her from a hell so personal she felt voyeuristic, as if she were looking in on someone else's nightmare.

He had a feeding tube down his throat; he couldn't swallow. His teeth were out, his face a sunken imitation of itself. When she kissed his cheek she had to stifle a gag reaction; his breath smelled like death. She put her hand on his forehead and stroked it, not knowing what else to do, not able to think of anything to say. Her touch silenced him; his eyes focussed intently on her face. He had stabilized, the doctor said. He could last months, maybe years. She wondered if Fern's pills could be dissolved somehow and poured into his tube.

Fern said hello, but then sat out of sight on a vinyl chair in a corner across from the bed. A shamefully consoling thought occurred to Eleanor. Knowing Andrew's pride, she thought maybe part of the desperation in his eyes had to do with not wanting her to see him in this state. Maybe she shouldn't have come.

She stood over his bed with her hand on his forehead until her bones started to ache. He hadn't looked away from her since she came in. Every few minutes his body became rigid in a sort of spasm, and she was reminded grotesquely of Dennis and Beth's old dog, Sport, lying ill in a corner of the kitchen, waiting to be put down. She pushed the image away, horrified.

"Andrew," she said. He was still watching her, afraid, it seemed, of her leaving. Those spasms. They couldn't just be happening for no reason. "Look upward if you want to say yes, and down for no," she told him. "Can you hear me? Do you understand?" He looked up, as if rolling his eyes skeptically. "Do you have any problem moving your eyes like that?" He looked down, almost closing his eyelids. "Very good," she said, feeling rather pompous. "Has anybody else thought of this way to communicate?" He looked down again. "The nurses? Your son?" He continued to look down. She thought maybe he just couldn't remember. She sat down on the chair by his bed. In a moment, his body became rigid with another spasm. "Andrew," she said, standing up again, afraid of the answer, "are you in pain?" He looked up.

Anxiety gripped her with nausea. She didn't have the strength for all this, the taking responsibility. She hoped his daughter would show up soon. Eleanor wanted to abdicate, to leave him alone to die, though she knew this was wrong. This wasn't the way she should feel. But the fact was, though he'd been her last love, he was not her husband. After forty-seven years, what happened to Orest had happened to both of them. This horror that was happening to Andrew was his alone. She could only watch it.

Orest had died of a heart attack while he was in the hospital after being diagnosed with stomach cancer. Pain was already eating at him before Eleanor was able to convince him to get any tests done. By the time he was sent back to the Kasokinaw hospital from Saskatoon, they both knew how his dying would be. He wanted to come home to the farm for a few more weeks, while painkillers in pill form could do something for him. But still in the hospital, he felt a vice gripping his chest, moving down his arm, and the nurses connected him to a heart monitor while they all waited for the doctor to return from dealing with a car accident in Mont Herbert. The monitor beeped off and on all day, though after that first panic, he felt no more symptoms. Eventually, everyone ignored the machine. He was sitting up in bed talking to Eleanor and Dennis just before the end of visiting hours, when it went off again. "Don't feel a thing," he'd said. "Goddamn contraption doesn't work right. Grant Devine sunk all the health-care money into grants so lawyers could build hot tubs in their backyards, and it's never recovered."

He died in his sleep that night. Answering the midnight phone call, Eleanor could feel nothing but relief. She sat in the dark letting the news sink into her pores, wanting to stay there all night within this peace, this blessed nothingness that now replaced the guarantee of so much misery. She felt as if she and Orest had won the lottery, and it took some time before she could grieve properly. She recalled walking into the church vestry at the funeral, greeting friends and family as if it were a potluck supper until she'd realized by their faces she'd better tone down the good cheer.

Andrew's son Gareth, a handsome hawk-faced man about Dennis's age, entered the room, hesitantly clearing his throat. When she and Fern first arrived, they'd chatted with him for a minute in the hallway outside Andrew's room, but then he'd gone for coffee. Eleanor hadn't seen Gareth since he'd moved to Vancouver in his early twenties. Back then he'd still had some baby fat. Now he was lean and fit, but she could see remnants of his boyhood. She could see he was bewildered, loose-limbed and listless with grief, bored silly and ashamed of it, the way men are when they can't do anything active to help. She knew how relieved he'd be to exchange this state for anger, so she was pleased she could direct it toward something of some use to his father. "Gareth," she said. "Did you know your dad can communicate by eye movements?"

"No! Really?" He was surprised, seemed somewhat confused.

"I've asked him to look up when he means yes, and down for no."

"But we tried something like that before, asked him to blink twice for yes, once for no. I guess he wasn't ready yet. Or he wasn't ready to cooperate."

Andrew was looking down. He looked at Gareth furiously, then looked down again to make his point. They were arguing, she realized. She had a brief urge to knock their heads together. "I just want to say I've found out he's in some sort of pain and you could maybe point this out to the nurses. If any of them were able to take even a moment's time, they should have noticed it by now. Here. See? It's happening again."

Gareth stood over him as he had another spasm. "Good lord."

"You see what I mean?"

"I thought that was just some muscular thing." He bent over the bed. "Dad. Dad," he said louder. "Are you in pain there?"

Fern was dozing in her chair, and Eleanor gently shook her shoulder. "Fern, we'll be going now." Gareth had pushed the call buzzer and was at the doorway, ready to capture the next nurse who walked by. Eleanor leaned over Andrew's bed to kiss his forehead. "We have to go now, my dear. I'll be back to see you soon." He rolled his eyes up practically into their sockets.

As Eleanor and Fern walked down the hall, they heard Gareth call, "Nurse." When nothing happened immediately, he yelled, "Nurse! For Christ's sake, my father needs someone here!"

She ran into Eston's son in the hospital lobby. "Mr. Eston." She held out her hand.

He stopped politely. "Mrs. Sawchuck."

"Eleanor." She didn't want to keep thinking of him as Eston. "And you're?"

"George."

"George." She paused awkwardly. "Next time you're in town, drop in for a cup of coffee."

She knew George would rather not see her again, and in fact, she thought, he was eyeing her rather reproachfully. He must recall her saying she wasn't long for this world. She should be here in the hospital all right, but on her deathbed.

"Yes," he said, moving away. He pointed outside to his wife pulling up in their Saturn. "My ride," he said, and left.

She hoped for his sake his father would soon be gone.

Eleanor was sick and tired. She took to her bed for several days with the flu, emerging weak and pale and barely able to stand. While she was sick, she'd phoned the hospital to leave a message for Andrew with his son, and found out his pain had been caused by a bladder infection from the catheter. It was now clearing up and he was much more comfortable.

She knew she couldn't leave Pleasant Manor for a couple of days yet and phoned the hospital again to talk to Gareth. "At my age," she said once she'd caught up on the particulars of Andrew's health and described her own, "I'm afraid the flu is no laughing matter." She wanted to make sure he impressed on his father her inability to visit right then.

"Yes. I mean, no, I'm sure it's not. Mrs. uh, Eleanor, here's the thing. I have to go back to Vancouver tomorrow. In a week Jeanie is flying in from Australia. Dad will be fine for a while, I'm not sure he wants to see any visitors anyway, you know what I mean? But, uh, that doesn't apply to you."

"Of course not," she said. "Well, I'll get there when I get there. You can tell him that, and give him my love."

There was a short silence. "I'll do that." He cleared his throat. "He's not in any pain now and this morning he moved his arm a bit, I'm thinking that might be a hopeful sign. I'm going to get some time off work. I'll be back in a couple of weeks."

"All right, Gareth. I'll see you then."

During Eleanor's illness, Mrs. Brown had sent an aide once a day to make sure she wasn't getting worse, to bring flu medicines and chicken soup, to help her wash. Dennis and Beth came every day too; Beth stayed a couple of nights, and Fern almost lived at Eleanor's place until she recovered. Eleanor was grateful to all of them, and for the company, though she and Fern spent most of the time reading or doing crossword puzzles in different rooms. Even on her best days, Fern needed to have her book lying on a stable surface in front of her, and Eleanor's desk was in her living room.

She was quite a bit better now, strong enough to go to the hospital if Fern came with her. Gareth had been gone for three days, and she was worried. She hoped Andrew understood she'd been ill, that she hadn't abandoned him. She would stop by Fern's and go to the Manor for lunch today; maybe she could ask Murray to drive them to P.A. that afternoon.

She stepped outside, feeling she hadn't been anywhere in months. It was a lovely day; it must be over seventy-five above. She stood on the walk in front of her door, letting the sun warm her. Her bleeding hearts and the ferns in her shaded garden plot had suddenly shot up. Maybe she should thin out the lilies of the valley. She looked up at the clear sky, grateful for the heat warming her blood, and thought of lizards on rocks, of alligators on mud beaches. People become cold-blooded as they age. She kept this thought to share with Fern, who would be glad to see her up and about.

She sat down on her lawn chair to rest, staring at her plants and thinking about Andrew, what his life must be like now, how he must long for death. Heartsick. The cliché was exact. Her heart felt sick for him, sick with pity, love and shame for hoping he'd die soon. Hoping not only for Andrew's benefit, but for her own, so she could get on with her life. At least he was too far gone for the second floor. He'd never have to put up with that particular hell.

Would she want to die if she had to live up there, senile people driving her mad? And what about other possibilities? Her own mind wasn't as sharp as it used to be. If she lasted into her nineties, she might be one of those driving others crazy. Or. What if she found herself living in close quarters there with Donald Eston?

Suppose, and she did suppose, that he was guilty of something. Even if he'd done only one of the atrocities described in the book, he was a monster. How did a person become like that? Did he start out that way? Were some people irredeemable from infancy?

Taking pleasure in hurting others seemed a common enough human frailty. Not that evil was frail. She pictured it as strong, sinuous, smashing or creeping its way through human existence. Well-meaning weaklings like her and Fern were the ones who embodied frailty.

And Andrew. What was happening to him was evil too. God-sanctioned, run-of-the-mill suffering. She was disgusted. Angry. She'd like to give God or Nature, the Universe or whatever, a good shake. Set things going properly.

She did not have to remain in Pleasant Manor for the remainder of her days. What she should do, rather than procrastinate until she was doomed to the second floor, was put herself on a waiting list for a care home in Prince Albert. Dennis could help her. If it weren't for Fern and

Olivia retiring here, she'd never have moved back to Kasokinaw in the first place.

Fern had a decent pension; she could move to P.A. with her. But what if their names came up before they were ready? What if she could still manage here in her comfortable suite and she suddenly had to choose: either move into a tiny, if private, room in a place like Extendicare, or stay and take her chances in Pleasant Manor? She looked down again at her garden plot and noticed a mat of chickweed. Everything that involved choice caused stress.

Right now she had to take hold of herself. Quit thinking, eat some lunch and prepare to go to P.A.

The curtain around the other bed in Andrew's room was drawn, cutting the room in half and giving it a draped, claustrophobic feel. She could tell he was feeling better: his eyes registered pleasure of recognition, although he moaned quietly and she had to grab one of the skimpy hospital tissues from his night table to wipe tears from his face. "I hope Gareth told you I was away with the flu." She waited until he confirmed this. "I've brought one of your books from home," she said, "to read to you?" He looked upward again, and she smiled at him, somewhat at a loss. Fern had stayed in the cafeteria for pie and coffee.

A nurse hurried in, giving the impression she was running a dash, ready to hand the baton over to another participant. She cranked the head of Andrew's bed up a bit and rolled him onto his side so he could see Eleanor when she sat down. She briskly opened the curtains around the other bed. "You all know each other," she announced, "though we're not sure how much Mr. Eston understands, or if he recognizes people. Since both of these gentlemen are from Pleasant Manor, they might give each other a bit of company." There lay Donald Eston, hunched on his side, his eyes tightly closed.

"Good lord." When she realized she'd said this aloud, a spasm — was it laughter? — weakened her knees and she sat down. She took a deep breath and looked up at the nurse, who was watching her with an unreadable expression. She made a couple of last adjustments to Andrew and left, saying she'd see them all later.

She stroked Andrew's forehead. "I brought Sherlock Holmes with me," she said. "Should I read an episode from *The Return*?" When he approved, she said, "I'll just be a couple of minutes. I want to say hello to Mr. Eston here."

Andrew looked down, a definite negative, but she made her way across the room to the other bed. "Mr. Eston." He continued to lie on his side with his eyes closed. "Donald." Saying his first name left her with a faint taste of something gone bad. She pulled a chair up to his bed, staring hard at him, examining his bushy eyebrows until he opened his eyes and looked at her. Their usual benign grey hardened, reminding her of cement, and for a confused second, she wondered if he might suddenly have gone blind.

"I know who you are," he said.

He had to be referring to Thelma's note. She continued to stare at him as a chill passing over her became colder, a winter stream flowing over her nerves. That note seemed so long ago now; a lifetime. "I don't know who you are at all." She didn't stop to consider what she was saying. "I read your daughter's book and I'm not sure if you're even human."

"I'm human all right."

"Did you do all that? What your daughter accused you of?"

For a long moment, he didn't say anything. "You'll only believe me if I say yes," he finally said. "Is that what you want?"

"I want to know the truth."

"The truth." He repeated the word as if it disgusted him. His eyes narrowed, seemed to look inward, as if remembering. "All right." He nodded his head, watching her. "Yeah. It's true, all of it and more, and what's it to you, to any of you croaking old bitches." Breathing heavily now, he looked away, and his expression regained its old blandness. Laboriously, he turned his back on her.

She stayed there another minute, not able to stand. She realized her hands were shaking and pressed them against her lap. Looking down at them, she noted how paper-like her skin seemed. She examined the back of the man's head with its fringe of hair on a skull spotted with age, and thought of his daughter, long dead. "I will tell your son what you just said," she told him. He didn't move.

She wondered if Eston had been given a sedative, wondered how difficult it would be to hold a pillow over his face. Death, of course, was a favour. If she were going to bestow it on anyone, it should be Andrew. But she knew she had neither the strength nor the courage. She was deficient in both love and hate and was wasting her own time thinking about it, for either of them.

Still shaking, she returned to Andrew's bedside. He seemed to be asleep, and although he'd been facing away from them, she wondered what he'd heard. She longed to talk to Fern. She anticipated the ride home and the drink they'd have at the end of this day as if she were a desert traveller nearing an oasis. Trying to compose herself, she opened the book she'd brought with her, but it might as well have been written in a foreign language.

About the Author

Marlis Wesseler has written four critically well-received books: the short-story collections *Life Skills* and *Imitating Art*, and the novels *Elvis Unplugged* and *South of the Border*. They have been finalists in various categories of the Saskatchewan Book Awards, including Book of the Year. An earlier version of *The Last Chance Ladies' Book Club* won a John V. Hicks Long Manuscript Award. After teaching school in Saskatchewan's far north and travelling extensively in her youth, Marlis moved to Regina, where she obtained an English degree, was a member of the writing group The Bombay Bicycle Club, worked on writing projects for Saskatchewan Education, reviewed manuscripts for a publishing house, and has sat on various literary arts boards and juries. She still lives and writes in Regina.

Eco-Audit
Printing this book using Rolland Enviro 100 Book
instead of virgin fibres paper saved the following resources:

Trees	Solid Waste	Water	Air Emissions
2	83 kg	6,767 L	273 kg